LONE STAR SILVER

**Center Point
Large Print**

**This Large Print Book carries the
Seal of Approval of N.A.V.H.**

LONE STAR SILVER

JACKSON COLE

CENTER POINT PUBLISHING
THORNDIKE, MAINE

This Center Point Large Print edition
is published in the year 2008 by arrangement with
Golden West Literary Agency.

The text of this Large Print edition is unabridged. In other
aspects, this book may vary from the original edition.
Printed in the United States of America.
Set in 16-point Times New Roman type.

ISBN: 978-1-60285-094-1

Library of Congress Cataloging-in-Publication Data

Cole, Jackson.
    Lone star silver / Jackson Cole.--Center Point large print ed.
        p. cm.
    ISBN 978-1-60285-094-1 (lib. bdg. : alk. paper)
    1. Hatfield, Jim (Fictitious character)--Fiction. 2. Texas Rangers--Fiction. 3. Texas--Fiction.
4. Large type books. I. Title.

PS3505.O2685L66 2008
813'.52--dc22

2007040397

Prologue

THREE men dreamed of wealth and power. Two, seated in a dimly lighted room in the border town of San Rosita, conversed earnestly in low tones. The third, lithe, sinewy, dark of face, with glittering black eyes and lank black hair, furtively forded the shallow Rio Grande and rode northward under the bright stars of Texas.

He glanced repeatedly to right and left and scanned the trail ahead. Riding slowly, ever watchful, he still did not see the silent figure that slipped along in the shadows just out of sight of the trail, a tireless figure that easily paced the steadily jogging horse.

In the dusky cabin room, lighted by but a single low-turned lamp, the two men spoke in guarded tones, despite shuttered windows and closed doors. One was tall and broad of shoulder. The other hunched grotesquely in his chair, the smoking lamp, behind and slightly to one side of him, casting his distorted shadow across the warped board floor.

From time to time the tall man glanced impatiently toward the door which he faced.

"He'd oughta be here any minute now," he growled. "Late now. Wonder if anythin's happened to him? He knows we're takin' a big chance, gettin' t'gether this way. Hadn't oughta keep us waitin'."

The other nodded, and raised his head suddenly at a slight sound outside the cabin. The other tensed, his eyes fastened on the door. The hands of both dropped out of sight beneath the table. Then both grunted with relief as the door swung outward on silent hinges and a dark, lithe man stepped carefully into the room lifting his booted feet high and setting them down gently before he turned to draw the door shut behind him.

"Bolt it!" the tall man shot at him. The newcomer nodded and slipped the rusty bolt under its rusty hasp. Drawing a third chair to the table, he sat down.

Young Dick Webb, Texas Ranger, slept lightly in his little room over the livery stable. Hardly had the echoes of a knock at the door died away before he was on his feet and slipping quietly across the room. As his hand reached for the knob, the knock was repeated. Webb's eyes snapped with excitement as he slipped the bolt and swung the door wide.

A sinewy, dark-faced little man slipped into the room and spoke in liquid Spanish—

"*He* crossed the river tonight."

"Cartina, you mean? Cartina, the bandit?" exclaimed Webb. "Where'd he go?"

"He is here," replied the other imperturbably.

"Here in San Rosita!"

"*Si!* He entered the old cabin that sits in the shadow of the bluff. A light burned within the cabin, and there were men inside. I saw before the door closed."

Dick Webb was hurriedly drawing on his clothes. He buckled his heavy cartridge belt into place with a snap, drew his Colt from its holster and slipped it back again, assuring himself that the action was smooth and free. The little man watched with beady eyes. Webb's face worked with eagerness.

"The chance I've been waiting for!" he exulted. "The chance to catch Cartina on this side the line. Pancho, you're making no mistake about this, I hope."

The little Yaqui tracker grunted.

"Meestake the man who slew father and mother?" he asked in broken English. "*Señor,* that ees not likely. Pancho knows! Pancho himself would have slain thees night, had not Pancho promised the tall *señor,* his friend. Pancho forgets not the great favor, the kindness."

"You've more than paid back the little thing I was able to do for you, Pancho," Webb declared earnestly. "This means one helluva lot to me, who's just got into the Rangers. Any man in the outfit would give his right arm to bag Cartina; and here's where I get him!"

He slapped his wide-brimmed hat onto his head and strode to the door.

"I go also?" questioned Pancho. "There is more than one?"

Webb shook his head. "No, Pancho," he said, "I think I can make out alone. You keep out of sight. The fact that nobody knows you're tied up with me is what makes you so valuable. If you went with me, it would tip your hand. You wait here for me."

Pancho said no more, but his dark countenance voiced silent disapproval. However, as the door closed, he squatted on his heels and rolled a cigarette with slender, nimble fingers.

7

It was less than three minutes' fast walk from the livery stable to the ramshackle old cabin by the bluff. The cabin, originally built by a wandering prospector, had long been deserted. It was seldom visited, even by children, and never at night. Crouched in the shadow of the steep bluff that overhung the trail, young Dick Webb surveyed it with eager eyes.

As he had said, Webb was new to the Rangers, and he was anxious to distinguish himself. He had been sent to San Rosita because of the raidings and killings of this very *Pedro Cartina,* the Mexican bandit, leader of a powerful and utterly merciless outfit. Cartina had defied the local authorities on both sides of the Line and even had routed a detachment of *El Presidente's rurales,* the efficient Mexican mounted police, which had been sent against him. The capture, lonehanded, of Cartina would be a feather in the cap of the oldest veteran of the Rangers. It would be a priceless boon to a recruit, the ink on whose commission was hardly dry.

Cautiously, Webb circled the cabin. He noted a front and rear door. It would not do to wait for Cartina to leave the shelter of the shack, for it was impossible to watch both doors at once and the Ranger had no way of knowing which the bandit would use. Cartina's horse was nowhere in sight, or Webb would have waited beside it. There was but one thing to do— tackle the cabin itself. Loosening his gun in its holster, Webb glided toward the front door. It opened outward, he saw, and doubtless was bolted on the inside.

Dick Webb was a big man and extraordinarily powerful. He had huge shoulders and muscle-packed arms. He saw that it was possible to slip his thick fingers between the warped door and the jamb, which it fitted imperfectly.

To do so was the work of an instant. With a mighty wrench he ripped the bolt screws from the wood and flung the door wide open. Gun in hand he leaped forward, and sprawled with a crash on the cabin floor, the Colt clattering across the room. A rope had been stretched across the doorway, ankle-high.

Webb rolled over on his side as the cabin seemed to fairly explode with the roar of six-shooters. He never had a chance. He died sprawled on the floor, his body battered and broken by bullets.

The bandit Cartina hissed words through the smoke.

"Out, *pronto!* Someone will have heard! Out, and away! We are agreed! Each knows what he is to do! Out!"

Boots clattered over the boards. The tall man and the Mexican vanished amid the shadows. The third man whisked the ponderous table from the floor as if it were made of straw and . hurled it at the guttering bracket lamp. There was a crashing of glass and hot oil spattered the floor. Flame flickered for an instant, then snuffed out in a cloud of evil smelling smoke. The man, seeing the failure of his plan for burning the cabin and thereby destroying all evidence of the killing, growled a curse and stumbled after his companions. A moment later fast hoofs drummed southward toward the Rio Grande.

Sheriff Branch Horton shipped the body of Dick Webb to Ranger headquarters at Presidio.

". . . and can't tell how it happened," the sheriff concluded his report. "Folks up the trail heard the shooting and reported it. All I could find was some cigarette butts—the kind greasers smoke—and horse tracks leading toward the river."

Stern old Captain Brooks had notions of his own, however. He made bitter exclamation and chalked up another murder against Pedro Cartina or some one of his outfit. He noted a peculiarity of the wounds in Webb's bullet riddled body.

"Not much to go on," he muttered to himself, "but it might mean something."

And the sardonic Gods of the Hills, looking down at the ant-like activities beneath their mountain tops, chuckled to themselves and warped another thread into the grim web that Death and Destiny were weaving back and forth across the silvery river.

Night over the Tamarra Valley, with the bright stars of Texas flaming like beacon lights on the towering crests of the gaunt Tamarra Hills. A lonely wind whispering through the blue grasses, and the Rio Grande a lovely silver mystery in the moonlight.

All the banks of the silver river were the purple pools of ragged-edged shadow, which marked the dense clusters of black willow, interlaced with scraggly button-bush. The hardy button-bush ventured even into the shallow water and seemed to reach tentative branches toward the dim Mexican shore. Welcoming branches, perhaps, extending an invitation to the moving shadows that flowed almost soundlessly into the murmuring water, and forged steadily toward the inquisitive button-bush and the willow screen.

The moonlight showed swarthy faces, lean sinewy bodies and the blue-gray glint of rifle barrels. Under the men and their guns were the blurry forms of tough little mountain mustangs with shaggy heads and dainty goat-hoofs. Five minutes later, the soft rustling and crackling among the willows ceased and those swift little hoofs drummed over the rolling rangeland of the Tamarra.

The gibbous moon swung low over the Tamarra Hills, faltered, seemed to hesitate and then slowly sank behind the glowering crags. For a moment the hill crests were outlined, grim and forbidding, against the wan afterglow. Then they softened to nebulous tracings on the star-flecked velvet of the sky.

Under that velvety, silver-jeweled sky, the great Slash K trail herd drowsed peacefully. The two night hawks riding herd silently blessed the docility of their long-horned charges. There was not a faint flicker of lightning along the horizon or a far distant mutter of thunder to disturb the tranquility of the cattle. Stomachs full of sun-sweet grasses of the great valley, the great beasts chewed ruminative cuds and allowed cattle-dreams to move sluggishly through their furry-edged minds.

The two cowboys, *their* stomachs full of steak, hot biscuits, sugary molasses, and other things equally delectable to puncher appetites, also drowsed comfortably in their saddles, their even-paced ponies moving slowly around the herd.

Beside the chuck wagon, the other Slash K punchers slept soundly, with nothing to disturb their slumbers. Nothing while the golden stars turned silver with the first faint kiss of the dawn.

And then—"lightning" flashed, "thunder" rolled and shrieking "rain" spattered the sleeping camp. But the lightning was the spurting fire from the black muzzles of unseen rifles, the thunder was the crash of the reports and the rain was a leaden rain of death.

The Slash K punchers by the chuck wagon died in their blood-sodden blankets—died without awakening from their sleep.

The two night hawks also went down under that first withering blast of fire, one drilled dead center with only a single spasmodic twitch left in his long body after it thudded to the ground. The other, crashing through a tangled clump of brush, came to rest with his bleeding head jammed against the gnarled roots, the low growing branches completely hiding him from view.

Silent and motionless he lay, while the band of swarthy-faced, yelling fiends got the great herd into motion and sent it thundering toward the Rio Grande.

Dizzy, shaking, he crawled forth as the clamor dimmed into the distance. A stumbling run to the bloody shambles that had been the camp quickly showed that he was the sole survivor of the raid. As the first light of dawn glowed softly over the crest of the eastern peaks, he caught a horse that had been overlooked, managed to crawl onto its bare back and set out for Presidio, where he knew there was a Ranger post. The sun was hardly an hour high before a compact body of Rangers was riding with loose rein and busy spur toward the spot where the silver band of the river marked the Texas Border.

"What are we going to do if we don't catch up with 'em before we reach the river?" a fresh-faced young Ranger asked of the tall, silent man who rode a splendid golden sorrel and led the troop. "Did Cap. Brooks say anything about us crossing the river, Hatfield?" he added.

The tall leader turned slightly in his saddle and favored the young Ranger with a level glance from his gray eyes. His lean, bronzed face was stern but there was a slight twinkle of humor in the strangely colored eyes.

"Well," he drawled, "he didn't say anything about us *not* crossing."

A murmur of approbation greeted the reply. The Rangers straightened in their saddle.

"Cap. McDowell did it in the old days," exclaimed one. "Brought his man back, too. We're with you, Jim. Whatever you say goes."

13

The man whom a taciturn old Lieutenant of Rangers had named the Lone Wolf, smiled at their enthusiasm, and that smile wrought a singular change in his stern face. His wide mouth quirked at the corners, his even teeth flashed white against his bronzed cheeks and his eyes grew sunny. The smile was fleeting as a shadow at sunset, however, and an instant later the mouth was a hard line and the eyes were as coldly gray as a snow-burdened wind sweeping under a leaden sky. Directly ahead was the silver shimmer of the Rio Grande, and beyond the wide river a rolling dust cloud fogged the clear crystal of the morning.

A buzz of exultation arose.

"It's them!" exclaimed the young Ranger, "and they're on the other side of the river!"

Hatfield glanced to right and left.

"I understand there's a ford right over by those cottonwoods," he remarked casually, swerving his tall sorrel.

The Rangers followed. In another moment they were surging through the shallow waters of the ford.

Once across the river, they gained rapidly on the scurrying dust cloud. Soon they were able to make out the undulating line of the herd. To right and left were riders who urged the tired cattle to greater effort. Hatfield's dark brows drew together as he estimated their number.

"Must be nearly a hundred of them," he muttered. "This is a pretty ambitious outfit. It must be Cartina, himself."

An angry hum arose at mention of the bandit-revolutionary's name. There was not a man of the outfit but who had his feud with the snaky-eyed, swarthy Cartina whose ruthless cruelty was a byword along the Border. Time after time the Mexican raider had swooped down onto Texas soil, left a line of robbery, arson and murder in his wake and dashed back across the river and into the mountains before organized pursuit could catch up with him and mete out the justice of the frontier.

The bandit was uncannily skillful in timing his raids and picking spots unguarded at the moment. The Tamarra Valley lived in terror of the clatter of his horses' hoofs and the thunder of his guns. Usually he operated toward the west end of the valley—seldom indeed did he come so far east as the scene of his present raid: it was too near the temporary Ranger post at Presidio. Doubtless the temptation of the great Slash K trail herd had proven too great.

"The devil's got brains," was the general verdict of the valley—"Brains and nerve, and no heart."

Jim Hatfield had caused silent old Captain Brooks to knit his white brows thoughtfully just a few days before.

"Uh-huh," Hatfield remarked, "he's got nerve—that's sure and certain, but brains? Maybe, and then again, maybe the brains belong to *somebody else!*"

Swiftly the Ranger troop closed the distance. Puffs of smoke from the dark figures riding beside the herd, and the whine of bullets, told them they were

15

observed. Hatfield eyed the dust cloud thoughtfully.

"There's too many of them for us to tackle head on, boys," was his verdict. "Hold back a bit and let's see what a little fancy shooting will do."

It did plenty! Saddles began to empty once the Rangers opened fire. The shrewd Hatfield gave another order—

"Hold back a bit more. I think our guns have got a longer range than theirs."

The order was obeyed and the results were immediate and salutary. Several more raiders were hit and return bullets kicked up puffs of dust yards in front of the troops. There was a wild milling among the Mexicans, a frantic waving of arms and a general disposition to seek shelter behind the terrified herd. Then order came out of chaos.

Hatfield saw a tall figure ride forward, another slighter one following closely; then the Mexicans stormed forward in a straggling body. They closed the distance quickly and bullets began whining about the Rangers. Hatfield immediately gave orders for retreat. The Rangers, on fresher horses, outdistanced the raiders, who finally halted and appeared to hold a conference. A moment later the two tall leaders detached themselves from the main body and rode away at a sharp angle. Hatfield watched them go, his eyes narrowing.

"That won't do," he told his men. "Those two are going for help. If they get it, they'll cut in behind us and get us between two fires; and that's liable to be uncomfortable.

"Haskins," he told a lean, grizzled Ranger, "you take charge of things. Keep after the herd and drive those horned toads off, if you can. If you get them on the run, turn the herd and head it back toward the river. I'll light out after those other two. Old Goldy won't have any trouble running them down. So long."

He spoke to the sorrel and crashed away in pursuit of the fleeing pair. As he had predicted, the tall golden horse gained steadily.

The pair were well mounted, however, and the bellowing herd was out of sight before he got in rifle range of the quarry. He could still hear the battle that was sweeping south, faintly crackling like dry sticks breaking or a winter fire popping.

"The boys are sure keeping them occupied," he chuckled, loosening his heavy Winchester in its scabbard.

Another ten minutes of hard riding and he was within shooting distance of the fleeing pair. His face set in grim lines, he reached for the rifle.

And then, the malignant hill gods decided to take a hand in this grim game whose stake was death. The flying sorrel put a foot into a badger hole, and got it out just in time to save himself a broken leg.

Not in time, however, to escape a prodigious tumble. Down he went, turned a complete somersault, rolled over and staggered to his feet, blowing and snorting. His rider lay where he had been thrown, silent, motionless, arms widespread, face to the sky.

The fleeing bandits, glancing over their shoulders

from time to time, saw the mishap. They pulled their horses to a halt, conferred a moment and then raced back to the fallen man. The sorrel saw them coming and trotted away, pausing at the edge of a grove. One flung a rifle and snapped a shot at the golden horse. The slug came close and Goldy, who had been shot at before and knew what to do, went away from there. The grove swallowed him up before the outlaw could fire again.

"Leave him be," growled the taller of the two. "We ain't got no time to fool with a stray cayuse."

Tense, watchful, guns ready for instant use, they approached the fallen Ranger. The slighter of the two, a sinewy, swarthy-faced man with snaky black eyes, slowly raised his rifle until his dark cheek snugged against the stock. His evil eyes glanced along the sights and drew a bead on the Ranger's breast. His companion reached out a big hand and shoved the rifle barrel aside.

"Wait," he rasped, "that's too easy! I got a better notion. Those meddlin' Rangers need a real lesson. We'll give 'em somethin' to think about when they come lookin' for this guy. Lay bolt of him and help me get him up in front of me. I know this section and a little ways ahead there's jest what we need. Wait. I ain't takin' no chances."

Drawing a black handkerchief from his pocket, he bound it about the lower portion of his face. When his broad-brimmed hat was pulled low, little could be seen but the glint of eyes in the hat brim's shadow.

Together they got the Ranger's limp form across the horse's back. For another mile they rode swiftly, paralleling the grove. Neither saw the golden sorrel pacing them in the shadow of the trees. When they halted at a sandy open space, the sorrel halted also, still under cover, and watched with great liquid wondering eyes all that went on.

He saw one of the outlaws cut four pegs from a stunted pinon pine that grew near the edge of the grove. He watched the pegs driven deep into the earth about a low mound. Then he saw the motionless form of his master stretched over the mound, his wrists and ankles firmly bound to the pegs with rawhide thongs taken from a saddlebag. Goldy did not know what it was all about, but he felt that something was very much wrong.

Jim Hatfield *knew* something was very much wrong when, a few minutes later, he regained consciousness from the shock of water being dashed into his face. He opened his eyes and blinked at the sun washed blue sky into which he was staring. His head ached and his whole body felt sore. About his wrists and neck was an unpleasant crawling sensation. He tried to jerk his hands down from their strained position and realized that they were firmly bound. He turned his head at the sound of a rasping chuckle.

Standing nearby, staring down at him were two men. One was slim and sinewy, swarthy of face, black of eye. The other, taller and broader than the first, was so masked by a black handkerchief and low drawn hat, the Ranger could make nothing of his face.

The tall man spoke, in a muffled, unnatural voice.

"Hope you and the ants have a nice time t'gether, feller," he said. "Mebbe yore Ranger pals will get here while they's still a little left of yuh, but it's sorta uncertain. The ants seem kinda hungry and they'd oughta get busy 'fore long. Yeah, yuh oughta have a nice time, pertickler when a ant runs in one empty eye socket and out the other, and yuh're still alive and kickin'. I've seed it happen 'fore now. Well, *adios*. Fellers that mess in Pedro Cartina's affairs usually wish they hadn't. Yuh won't be the fust."

The dark-faced man chuckled and turned to his horse, which was standing nearby. The other did not chuckle. He glared down at the Ranger with burning, hate-filled eyes for a moment. Then his glance faltered, turned aside from the Ranger's answering stare, came back, and wavered away once more. Growling curses back of the mask, he strode forward, kicked the prostrate man viciously and then whirled to join his companion. A moment later hoofs clicked away into the distance.

High in the sun-golden sky, a black shape whirled and hovered. Another joined it, and another, and another. They planed lower, staring with telescopic eyes that could see the ants streaming from the disrupted hill. Stared, and croaked dismally. The vultures knew that when the ants had finished, little would be left for them, and even their cold courage shrank away from the vicious little killers of the dark tunnels and passages underground.

For long moments Jim Hatfield lay staring into the hot sky. Despite the sunlight he felt cold, cold with a horror that left his body clammily moist and the hair prickling at the back of his neck. There are many ways in which a man may die, but few so frightful as being slowly eaten alive by the voracious ants. Hatfield had seen what was left of victims who had endured the torture of the ants and died screaming an agonized welcome to death.

With all his strength he tugged at the unyielding rawhide, cutting his wrists cruelly. Already he could feel the slow crawl of the questing insects, as yet merely curious as to what was this monster who had crushed their hill. Soon, he knew, they would scent blood and begin their carnage. Panting with effort he relaxed his straining muscles, his mind racing at top speed, seeking for the avenue of escape that did not exist. He writhed at the first stinging bite. His wrists were bleeding and the scent of the fresh blood was maddening the ants.

He strained his ears to a sound that came to him along the ground and for a moment a wild thrill of joy coursed through his veins. The sound was the beat of hoofs. Perhaps his companions, sensing his danger, were hurrying to the rescue. Then a plaintive whinny sounded and he realized the source of the hoof beats. It was the sorrel, coming to his master, perplexed at his strange position.

For a moment the pang of destroyed hope left the Ranger sick and weak. With an iron effort of the will he shook the feeling off, pursed his lips and whistled to the sorrel. Goldy answered with another whinny, padded up to the hill and thrust his damp muzzle into his master's hand. Hatfield managed to touch the friendly, inquiring nose with his fingers, and found comfort in the contact. The horse might be of no help, but his very presence was something.

Goldy nuzzled the hand, blowing softly, nipping Hatfield's fingers with gentle teeth.

"God, Goldy, if you could only chew that rawhide!" the Lone Wolf breathed. "It's no use, though—that's too much to expect of any hoss."

Goldy snorted questioningly and nuzzled again at the Ranger's hand. Again he nipped, with velvety lips, champing his bit, slobbering over the constraining steel. Hatfield's hand and wrist were wet. So was the peg against which it was bound, and so was the rawhide thong. Goldy continued to nuzzle.

The ants were biting freely now. Hatfield writhed despite his iron control and cursed softly through his set teeth. Again he tugged with all his strength, arching his body with effort, slicing the flesh of his wrists.

With a mad thrill of joy, he felt that his right hand moved the merest trifle. Yes, he was sure of it! It was not so close against the peg now. He redoubled his efforts, and the hand moved a little more.

Suddenly, the solution of the mystery burst upon

him. The nuzzling, slobbering horse was wetting the rawhide thong—*and rawhide stretches when wet!*

Hatfield began talking to the horse, softly, persistently, using all the endearing terms he had ever employed toward the intelligent animal. Goldy blew his appreciation and continued to nuzzle the hand whose fingertips caressed his nose. Abruptly he started back with an explosive snort. An ant had crawled into his nostril, and had bitten him. He blew prodigiously and backed away a pace.

Hatfield's voice rose, urgent, insistent. The dubious horse hesitated, fidgeted on restless feet, and thrust his muzzle back into the caressing hand. Hatfield strained with every atom of his magnificent strength. Goldy nipped at his hand.

Again the sorrel reared away, snorting with indignation. A score of ants had crawled upon his nose. He shook them off and eyed his prostrate master reproachfully. Hatfield put forth his strength in one final terrific effort. The planing vultures dropped lower. The black shadow of one rested on the Ranger's face for a fleeting instant—rested like the cold shade of Death's reaching hand. Hatfield gave one last desperate lunge.

The stubborn rawhide yielded, held, yielded a trifle more as the moisture reached the inmost fiber, yielded again, and the loosened loop flipped over the head of the stake!

Hatfield twisted over on his side, gripped the stake that held his left hand and tore it from the ground. He sat up, ripped free the thongs that held his ankles and staggered to his feet. Instantly he fell headlong, so numbed were his limbs. On hands and knees he crawled away from the terrible hill. Again he got to his feet, beating the ants from his clothing. The vultures croaked their disappointment, spiraled high into the sky and drifted away in search of easier prey. Hatfield shed the last of the ants, freed his wrists and ankles from the thongs and shambled to his horse.

"Thanks, Goldy," he said quietly, and the golden horse seemed to understand.

Swinging into the saddle, the Ranger galloped back toward where he had left his troop. Before he reached the spot, he saw the dust cloud boiling against the sky. But this time it was rolling north. A little later he could make out the toiling herd. The Rangers were driving it toward the Rio Grande, meanwhile fighting a rear guard action with the disheartened Mexicans.

Three of their number were wounded when Hatfield reached them, none seriously. His deadly rifle was an added inducement for the Mexicans to give up the fight. Soon the silver river shimmered in the sunlight and the pursuit fell back. A score or more cowboys were riding along the northern bank. Others were urging their horses into the water. That night the Slash K trail herd, heavily guarded by watchful punchers, was again on its way to market.

"Fine work, son," white-haired old Captain Brooks told the Lone Wolf, "as fine a piece of Ranger work as I've seen in many a day. Captain McDowell is going to be prouder than ever of you when I write him about it."

He stroked his snowy beard with a hand whose thinness and pallor still bespoke the ravages of recent illness. He did not appear over-pleased with what he had to say next, and his voice held a regretful note when he spoke.

"Got news for you," he said. "You'll probably be glad to hear it—gladder than I am to tell you. You're transferred back to McDowell, effective today. I'm over my sick spell and strong enough to take charge of things at this post again, and Cap. Bill is anxious to have you back with him, particularly since he's at the new post in El Paso county, 'way over west. I hear there's trouble brewing over on the Salt Flats, and along that new railroad they're building. McDowell probably has plenty for you to do; but I'll hate to lose you, son. You certainly have handled things first rate since you took over here while I was on the sick list. Yes, sir, I hate to lose you."

Hatfield nodded, staring somberly out of the window toward the grim Tamarra Hills.

"I'm not so glad as I thought I'd be, sir," he said. "Of course I like getting back with my own outfit— that's just natural—but I sort of hate to be leaving here right now. I'd like to have another crack at those two men who turned me over to the ants. And it seems, sir, that there are some funny things going on in this valley these days."

Old Captain Brooks was slow in replying.

"Yes," he said at length, "yes, there is—almighty funny. There's some mighty sinister influences at work hereabouts, son. Powerful influences that have to be reckoned with. The sort of thing that doesn't belong in Texas, or anywhere else in America, for that matter. Mark my word, son, there are bitter days in store for this state if certain folks get where they can have the whole say. What's goin' on in the Tamarra Valley will spread all over the state. It's got to be stopped."

"Maybe the Rangers can take a little hand in the stopping," suggested Hatfield.

Brooks slowly shook his white head.

"It's the Rangers who are liable to be stopped," he predicted soberly. "Mark my words—this post at Presidio isn't going to last. It'll be abandoned before the year is out."

"But, sir," exclaimed the surprised Ranger, "there isn't a district where a post is needed worse, what with Cartina and those other outlaws down below, and the Comanches to the north. Why—"

"Those things won't be allowed to count," Brooks interrupted. "The Rangers are the one organization certain folks are scared of. The Rangers can't be bought, and they can't be scared. The only thing is to get them out of the way. That'll be the move, see if it isn't. And if *he* gets to be governor, like he's planning on, in a mighty short time they won't be any Rangers—the outfit will be disbanded and a mighty different sort of outfit will be riding over this state."

"*He* ought to be stopped, sir."

"Uh-huh. But so far as anybody can see, he doesn't ever do anything that is a real law violation, and that's the only thing the Rangers can act on. John Chadwick's a law abiding citizen if there ever was one. It's just that in this valley he comes mighty close to *being* the Law!"

"And that kind of Law has no place in Texas, or America, sir."

"No, it hasn't, son. It certainly hasn't. Well, I guess it's something for wiser heads than you and I to worry about. We have our own work to do. So, you head back to McDowell in the morning. Somebody else'll do the job of runnin' those rustlers down. They won't last much longer. You think one was Cartina, all right?"

"Pretty sure the smaller one was Cartina," the Ranger replied.

"And the other one?"

"Can't say *who* he was—had his face covered up—but I've got a good notion of *what* he was."

"Huh? *What* he was?" repeated the surprised Captain. "Well, what?"

Hatfield fixed him with his level gray eyes, his voice was soft and steady.

"*The brains!*" he replied.

Chapter I

WESTWARD across the Tamarra Valley from the desert's edge, a range of gaunt hills shouldered the brassy-blue Texas sky. There was nothing beautiful about them. Scantily clothed with sparse, dry vegetation, their slopes, fanged with boulders, and seamed by watercourses, straggled upward toward a sheer wall of craggy cliffs that formed their crest. In the shadow of those towering cliffs the slopes were darkly blue and somberly mysterious, and there seemed to be a concealed threat in the deep gorges with their shadows.

Farther down the slopes, the rocks and earth were splashed with gold and the gnarled trees burned pale amber in the hot shimmer of the afternoon sunshine. Water sounded in the gorges, water that leaped over black rocks or hissed smoothly against canyon walls.

Very silent were the hills, save for the sound of the water and the restless whimper of the wind in the burr oaks and pinon pines.

It was a crouching sort of silence. It was the silence of watching eyes and listening ears, and a poised threat.

"Threatening" described it best of all. The gaunt hills wore the silence as an executioner wears his black robe, wrapping it about their shadowy shoulders, with the tattered fringe trailing away toward the sun-drenched plain.

Ed Shafter, trudging across the gold and emerald sweep of the Tamarra, his gray old burro following him, sensed the ominous silence even as he crossed the sun spangled rangeland toward the hills.

His eyes narrowed as they swept the gray loom of the hills and the big muscles of back and arms swelled under his patched coat. For a moment his whole long, lean body was tense. Then he shrugged his wide shoulders, laughed a little in his beard and lengthened his stride. He hoped to camp in some sheltered draw at the base of the hills, where wood and water would be plentiful.

"Ought to be able to knock over a rabbit or a couple blue grouse," he told the burro. "That'll sort of change my diet off from bacon and beans. Oh, I know, *you* don't care, you scraggle-tailed old grass burner, but *I* crave chuck that's a little different now and then. C'mon, 'fore I leave you out here to grow roots and turn into a loco weed!"

The burro wagged a contemplative ear and did not appear particularly impressed; but he quickened his pace a bit to keep at the heels of his tall master.

Ed Shafter was forty years old and looked sixty. Gray streaked the brown beard that hung over his arching chest and spread out almost to his wide shoulders. There was gray in the hair that escaped from beneath his ragged hat, and what could be seen of his face was deeply lined. His blue eyes were clear and bright. He was long of limb, stringy of muscle and his every movement was assured.

The clothes he wore were a weird patchwork, the original base of which had been faded blue overalls, blue woolen shirt, coat of some nondescript dark color and black slouch hat. Now there were more patches than base, even patch upon patch, running the gauntlet from rawhide to rabbit skin. His boots were also carefully patched and sound of sole. A heavy six-gun sagged on his right hip and the rough handle of a Bowie knife protruded from one boot top. Crooked in his arm was a Winchester.

The sun was still peering over the hill tops when Ed Shafter left the prairie and began toiling up a long dry wash whose sides were green with grama grass and splashed and starred with flowering weeds. The floor of the wash was studded with water-rounded boulders and littered with fragments casually, but his chief interest seemed centered on the ragged rim of the wash, and on the marbled ledges that flung up at its head. He appeared to be a prospector with a definite goal in view, with no time to waste on dubious surface indications.

That he was a wandering prospector, a typical desert rat, it seemed there could be little doubt. Pick and shovel peeped from the burro's pack. A chipping hammer was also in evidence.

As Shafter neared the head of the wash, he proceeded more slowly. Several times he paused, as though listening for something and his gazed roved backward and forward along the irregular ledges ahead. He could see now that the wash turned sharply and was really but the entrance to a deeper gorge that slashed the hills. His dark brows drew together at the discovery and he muttered something back of his bearded lips. He began to examine the ground carefully.

Suddenly he paused. His eye had caught the gleam of deep mineral stains on a bit of float. He picked up the stone and examined it with growing excitement. Beard and moustache pursed together in a soundless whistle. Shafter raised his eyes to stare unbelievably at the beetling breast of the hills. He shook his head in a dazed unbelief. Again he glanced at the stone, read its story with a trained mining man's practiced glance. The evidence in his bronzed hand was indubitable.

Again he raised his eyes to the unpromising battlements of those forbidding hills. Still shaking his head, he strode onward, and a moment later picked up another piece of float, and in another moment a third. Shafter halted, and stared at the mineral fragments, his face working. Again his glance sought the hill crest, and again he incredulously shook his head.

Silver in the Tamarra Hills! Silver of a richness vouched for by the bits of float borne down the draw by turbulent storm water! It just couldn't be! Spaniard Conquistadore, scout, emigrant, cattleman, wandering prospector—all had passed the forbidding range, giving the grim crags and battlements a wide berth. Only the marauding Apache, the fleeing outlaw, the furtive smuggler sought sanctuary amid the cliffs and canyons and gloomy caves.

"Somebody might have dropped them rocks out of a pack or somethin'," Shafter declared to his burro. But his voice held no conviction. The miner in him knew that the mineral-packed float had been torn loose from some ledge farther up the draw.

Sunset was flaming in all its scarlet and gold and shimmering bronze glory when Ed Shafter made his camp near the head of the draw. And as he boiled his coffee and fried his bacon, Destiny shuffled through the prairie grasses to the east and Death drifted silently across the purple-silver ribbon far to the south that was the stately Rio Grande.

Shafter could not hear those dragging footsteps through the grasses nor the muffled plod of hoofs up the muddy river bank, but a cold wind fanned his face and he hunched closer to his little fire, his mind brooding over twin problems. From time to time he drew a crumbling fragment of float from an inner pocket and stared at the blue threads that were silver. After each examination he would raise his eyes and gaze toward that shadowy river far to the south, and the muscles of his lean jaw would quiver beneath the beard. Finally he fumbled within his shirt, touching something there with his bronzed, sinewy fingers. As if by magic, the indecision left his steady eyes and with a shrug of his broad shoulders he dropped the bit of float back into his pocket, nodded purposefully toward the unseen river and prepared his bed.

And Destiny and Death drew nearer.

Chapter II

MORNING came and Shafter, tired out by a long and hard trudge across the rangeland, slept late. The sun was high behind a sullen veil of clouds as he cooked his breakfast and ate it leisurely. He was washing his few dishes when his keen ears caught the sound that drifted up the draw.

There was a patient clicking of little hoofs on stone, and another sound, a dragging shuffle that kept laborious time with the first.

"Burro comin' t'other side that brush, and a man," Shafter deduced. "Man walks like he's hurt," he added, listening to the hesitant shuffle.

Picking up his rifle he cradled it negligently in his arm, where it could be swung into instant action should occasion warrant. Then he lounged carelessly in the shadow of a gnarled burr oak, where he could see better than he could be seen. There was something menacing about that indecisive shuffle. Shafter felt it, but was at a loss to explain why.

Abruptly he relaxed, an exclamation on his lips.

Through the final fringe of the growth, a man had appeared, a man and a burro. The burro was a sturdy little animal, loaded with a well arranged pack. The man was the strangest individual Shafter had ever seen.

Wide, thick shoulders hunched high about the massive neck, powerful, simian arms dangling loosely, ending in finely shaped hands with slim, tapering fingers that hung well below his knees. He was not over five feet tall. His legs were bowed and crooked and worked stiffly from the hips, giving him a peculiar shuffling gait that dragged feet singularly small for the rest of him. His body was unutterably grotesque, utterly misshapen, vibrating crude physical power.

"Those arms could crack a hoss's ribs, and he could come darn near gettin' em' around a hoss, too," muttered Shafter, staring amazedly at the face so out of place on that distorted form.

As grotesque as the stranger was in body, he was beautiful of face. The pushed-back *sombrero* revealed crisply curling hair golden as the evening sunlight, a broad, finely shaped forehead, delicately curved dark brows that shaded eyes as clearly blue as a summer sky. The nose was straight with sensitive nostrils. The mouth was wide but with perfectly formed lips above a prominent, determined chin. It was a proud, sensitive, intelligent face.

The hunchback carried no rifle, but twin holsters swung from his heavy double cartridge belts, one holster worn slightly higher than the other. He paused a dozen paces distant from the tall bearded man, bowed courteously and spoke.

"Buenas dias, señor," he said in a voice that was like the music of the waters echoing from the soundboard of the hills.

"Mawnin'," replied Shafter, concealing his surprise

34

at the other's Spanish greeting. The man certainly did not look Mexican.

The hunchback spoke again, in unaccented English that was free of the soft drawl and slurred word endings that characterizes the Southwest.

"I smelled your coffee," he said. "Been out myself for two days," he added with a flash of white, even teeth.

Shafter chuckled his understanding.

"It shore is tough, especially if you're sorta used to havin' it reg'lar," he admitted. "Amble up here and set. Pot's still nigh onto half full. I made plenty this mawnin'."

He stopped to stir the embers together as he spoke. He straightened with his back to the other and stood, lithe and tall as a young pine of the forest.

Into the hunchback's blue eyes suddenly came a murky light of intense bitterness. His unbelievably handsome face contorted and for a moment its marvelous beauty dimmed as does the bright loveliness of the prairie under the shadow of a storm cloud. Then, as Shafter turned, the light died, the cameo-perfect features smoothed and the eyes became clear again.

"Thanks," he accepted the offer.

Before he squatted beside the fire, however, steaming tincup in hand, he slipped the pack from the burro's back and dropped it to the ground. Shafter liked him for that little act of thoughtfulness. His shrewd eyes ran over the outfit.

"Prospector?" he asked.

The hunchback nodded.

"No luck," he volunteered in answer to the unspoken question in the other's eyes. "Thought I'd work up through the Tamarra Hills and over to the Huecos, maybe. I've a notion there ought to be something worth while up there."

"Know the country?" Shafter asked.

"Fairly well," the other replied. "My ancestors owned most of it at one time. They lost title when the courts invalidated the old Spanish grants in this section."

His blue eyes hardened slightly as he spoke.

In Shafter's was a light of understanding. "You come down from one of the old Spanish families, then?"

The question was really a statement. The other nodded.

"Yes," he replied quietly, "I'm a Capistrano— Amado Capistrano is my name."

"And I callate you're entitled to write *Don* 'fore the Amado, if you take a notion," observed Shafter.

Amado Capistrano shrugged with Latin eloquence.

"It would be rather out of place before a desert rat's name, don't you think?" he replied.

"Not necessarily," answered Shafter, gazing thoughtfully at the proud sensitive face. With instinctive tact he changed the subject.

"Yore folks used to own the rangeland down there?" with a wave of his hand toward the lovely Tamarra Valley.

"Yes," the other replied. "John Chadwick owns it now. Know him?"

"Heard of him," Shafter replied.

That was not very definite. Almost everyone in that section of Texas had heard of John Chadwick, the cattle king. Chadwick was reputedly very wealthy, had served a term as State Senator and was spoken of as a possible candidate for governor.

Capistrano finished his coffee and stood up.

"Thanks," he said again, lifting the pack to the burro's back. "Guess I'll head on up the draw."

A little later Shafter watched the other man's grotesque form shuffle toward the wide mouth of the gorge. At the end of the wash he hesitated, apparently doubtful whether to turn to the right or the left, and as he paused, Destiny cast the dice. There was a flutter of grayish white, a skittering among the stones as a cottontail rabbit darted from a covert, weaved erratically for a moment and then sped away to the right. Shafter could almost hear the hunchback's amused chuckle as he too turned to the right and vanished up the gorge.

Late afternoon found Shafter on the move. He entered the gorge, drove straight ahead for a mile or two and then veered slightly to the left. Suddenly he paused, his eyes narrowing.

Directly ahead a ledge of grayish rock, marbled with black and yellowish blotches, undulated along the dark side of an abrupt rise. Shafter eyed it, breathing deeply. He strode forward with long strides, paused, loosened his prospector's pick from the burro's pack and sank it into the rock. It came crumbling down in brittle lumps.

With a trembling hand, Shafter picked up one of the fragments. It was streaked and veined with silver. He examined another, and another. Each was as the first—unbelievably rich in silver ore.

Shafter straightened up, his eyes blazing. Clenching the stones in sweat-moistened hands he stared at the ledge, turned abruptly and gazed toward the south. Lips tight, he dropped the bits of ore into his pocket, carefully scuffed dirt over the remaining fragments, smeared dust on the fresh scar his pick had left and resolutely turned his back on the ledge. He turned sharply to the left and strode southward with long strides.

And several miles to the north, the hunchback descendant of the Conquistadores paused before the face of a sheer cliff, sighed wearily and, turning, retraced his steps, veering more and more to the left as the shadows lengthened.

As the blue dusk was descending on the hill tops, Shafter made a fireless camp less than half a mile from the precipitous slope that was the south wall of the gorge. In the shadow of an overhanging rock he sat silent, motionless, rifle across his knees, eyes fixed on a wide notch that cut the gorge wall. From this notch flowed a ribbon of trail, or what passed for a trail. Shafter, who, like Amado Capistrano, was fairly familiar with the country, knew that it was the sinister Huachuca Trail that writhed its bloodsplotched way northward from the purple mountains of Mexico.

Silently he watched the gloomy notch, while a great white moon soared up over the eastern rim of the world and edged the black velvet of the hills with silver.

The moon climbed higher, bathing the gorge in ghostly light, and still the bearded Shafter sat motionless, alert.

Suddenly he stiffened, his lean hands gripping the rifle. Eyes eager, he leaned forward.

There was motion in the notch—furtive, indistinct motion that quickly became clearcut and real. Shadowy forms bulked large and grotesque in the wan moonlight.

Tense, quivering with excitement, Shafter watched them jolt down the trail—the mounted men, the loaded mules. Even at that distance he could recognize the long, deadly looking cases and the chunky boxes that seemed to swell with lethal power. His breath came quick and fast.

"I was right!" he muttered. "It wasn't a loco yarn of a drunken greaser! Nobody but me b'lieved it, but I was right! They're doin' it! They're gettin' ready! This is big! And nobody but me caught on to what was happenin'!"

His whole attention riveted on the stream of men and beasts flowing down the distant trail, he failed to see his gray old burro shuffle up a little rise and stand outlined clear and distinct in the moonlight.

For long minutes Shafter watched the ghostly caravan slide through the notch and vanish amid the shadows of the gorge. When the last outrider disappeared, he straightened his cramped limbs, stood up and strode out of the shadow. He turned quickly, gripping his rifle, at a slight sound behind him. Not ten paces distant stood a form blending into the shadows. A shaft of moonlight bathed the face, outlining every feature.

For a paralyzed second Shafter stared, his face that of a man whose judgment and trust has been shattered. Then he read the message in the eyes glaring into his, he flung his rifle to his shoulder. The other's hands moved with blinding speed.

Ed Shafter died with his finger squeezing the trigger of his rifle. Died under the blast of lead belching from two blazing guns, black holes blotching his broad forehead. He crumpled back in the shadow of the overhanging rock, a shapeless bundle of patched clothes, almost hidden from view. The killer deliberately fired twice more. He was taking no chances. A moment later he shot the old burro.

The white moon slid down behind the western crags. The stars dwindled to pin points of pale flame before they vanished in the whitening vault of the sky. The silent dawn spread its red mantle over the lonely mountains. The sun rose in gold and scarlet splendor and it was day.

Other days came, gray days and golden days, and moon bright nights and nights of lashing rain and wailing winds. Summer gave way to Autumn. And still the huddled bones of Ed Shafter lay in their moldering rags under the overhanging rock.

Strange sounds came to the hill country—unwonted thunders, mysterious boomings that puzzled the coyotes and sent the owls winging away. Also a low growl and mutter that swelled and lessened, rose and fell, but never ceased.

Two wandering miners discovered Shafter's skeleton. They stared at the grisly remains, bent over them gingerly. One pointed to the holes in the fleshless skull. The other nodded, bending closer as a gleam of metal caught his eye. With a hesitant hand he fumbled the tattered shirt, jerking loose the shining object pinned to the rotten undershirt beneath. He held the bit of silver in his horny palm and he and his companion stared at it with dilated eyes.

"Bill," he said, mouthing the words nervously, "this ain't no ord'nary killin'. Yuh know what *this thing* stands for. We'd better hustle down to town and report this. Sheriff's purty apt to be there—spends more time in Helidoro now than at San Rosita, the county seat."

The other shifted uncomfortably.

"Curt," he objected, "we hadn't oughta be havin' no truck with that sheriff, not after that run-in we had with him last week. I don't hanker to go reportin' no killin' to him. Can't tell what might be liable to happen."

The first speaker considered.

"Mebbe yuh're right," he admitted, "but jest the

same this'd oughta be reported—I won't feel right if it ain't. Them fellers is square shooters and they ain't nobody got no bus'ness pluggin' 'em. Tell yuh what. Franklin ain't sich a turrible ja'nt fer fellers like you and me—hardly a hundred miles. S'posin' we jest amble over there and report to the post?"

"Now yuh're talkin', feller," his companion agreed heartily. "That's jest what we'll do."

He glanced about with keen eyes, calculating distances, noting landmarks. He nodded toward the Huachuca Trail sliding furtively through the notch.

"Got the place all easy marked for the tellin'," he said with satisfaction. "I can lay 'er out so a blind man with the shakin' palsy can find 'er. C'mon, podner, stretch yore laigs."

Chapter III

RARELY does rain fall upon the Tamarra Desert, that grim waste of alkali, scrub and dust powdered sage which stretches from the Huecos to the Tamarra Hills. But when it does rain, it is as if the floodgates of the heavens were opened. And always, before the first hissing lances spatter the gray leaves of the sage, a roaring wind swirls the choking alkali dust in blinding clouds that blot out the sun and fill the air with a rasping grit.

Nothing lives in the Tamarra Desert, not even a callous snake or hardened lizard. The wolf and the coyote give it a wide berth and seldom do even the vultures sail over the dreary expanse. Only when some ill-advised wanderer gets caught in a storm do they appear.

How do they know the lost one is there? Perhaps they hear the Hill Gods chuckle, even above the roar of the storm. Doubtless they were whetting their beaks in anticipation as they peered down with telescopic eyes, that could perhaps pierce the dust clouds, at the man who struggled blindly across the dismal waste, gasping, choking, bending his head to the beat of the winds, reeling drunkenly from time to time.

He was a little man, dark of face, scrawny of body, clad in a greasy shirt and pantaloons, rope sandals, tattered *serape* and floppy straw *sombrero*.

Hugged to his breast, a rag wrapped around the lock to protect it from the dust, he held a shiny new rifle.

Through all his bitter battle against the storm he grimly clutched the heavy weapon, even when he tripped over some unseen straggle of sage or scrub and fell, which was often. He still held onto it when for the last time he crashed to the earth, writhed feebly for a moment and was still, while the dust drifted and settled upon his unconscious form.

Farther south and to the west another man fought the storm, a tall man mounted on a splendid sorrel horse. The sorrel's glorious golden coat was streaked and smeared with the gray dust, his ears and his mane were furred with it, but he held his head high and snorted defiance to the stinging clouds. With rare instinct he avoided the snarls of sage and scrub, planting his hoofs daintily on the yielding silt. North by east he forged ahead, the wind blasts ruffling his tail and tossing his mane, apparently untired despite the hundred miles he had put behind him in the past two days.

The rider was as noteworthy as the horse he rode. Tall, broad of shoulder and lean of waist and hip, he rode with the easy grace of one born to the saddle. His hair, where it was not dusted with the gray alkali, was crisp and black. His face was lean and bronzed with a wide mouth and level gray eyes.

Those eyes were the most striking feature of the man's face. To oldtimers they called to mind other eyes, the eyes of men who had walked through the smoke-misted West with courage—unafraid; in whose presence other men were wont to speak softly and move their hands with care.

"All steel and hickory and coiled-up chain lightnin'," a critical observer would have said, "and when he goes after those two guns, there's nothing for the other fellow to do but die gracefully!"

The two guns hung low in carefully worked hand-made holsters, their long barrels tapping against the rider's muscular thighs, the black butts flaring away from his lean hips. A heavy Winchester swung in the saddle boot.

Through the clouds of dust there suddenly came the hissing deluge of icy rain. The sorrel snorted explosively at the sting of the water, but the rider grunted relief.

"Don't be kicking, oldtimer," he admonished, "it'll lay this dust, and that's something to be thankful for. My lips are cracked open and my eyes feel as though I'd been rubbing sand in them. And I guess you're in about the same fix. This'll wash us off and make us feel a big sight better—you see if it doesn't!"

The sorrel snorted again, and shook his head as if in disagreement. Abruptly he shied, jolting his rider by his unexpected sideways leap.

"Easy, Goldy," growled the man. "What's eating you?"

The sorrel snorted again, capering nervously and rolling his eyes toward a low mound which appeared to be just another dust-covered clump of sage.

Jim Hatfield had long ago learned to trust the instinct of his big mount. Anything that appeared out of the ordinary to Goldy, he had learned, would bear investigation. The tall Ranger Lieutenant halted the sorrel, quieted him with a soothing word and gazed at the silent mound with speculative eyes. He could just distinguish its outlines through the rain, which was now descending in wind-whipped sheets.

Lithely he swung to the ground, shaking the water from the brim of his hat. A long stride and he reached the motionless form. Another instant and he was kneeling beside it, brushing away the sodden dust, to reveal a dark-faced little man who lay limp, something clutched to his scrawny chest. It was a task to break his grip on the heavy rifle with its rag wrapped lock.

For an instant the gun drew Hatfield's attention from the man. He examined it with growing curiosity, recognizing it as a latest model United States Army rifle. His gaze shifted back to the man.

"Now where in blazes did a little half starved Mex get hold of a gun like *this?*" he wondered. "Got about as much business with it as a hog with a hip pocket!"

He felt of the unconscious man's heart, found that it beat with fair strength.

"Just knocked out by the dust and heat," he decided. "He ought to snap out of it before long. The rain'll help. I'd better get him to some place where I can make a fire. Hot coffee will be just the thing when he comes to."

He picked up man and rifle with no apparent effort. Just as easily he mounted, cradling the limp form in front of him. He spoke to the sorrel and the big horse moved on, evidently as little affected by the burden as was his master. Another hour of battling the rain and the wind and they struck the first slopes of the Tamarra Hills.

In a sheltered canyon, beneath the overhang of a tall cliff which formed a perfect protection from the rain, Hatfield built a fire. The little Mexican still lay silent, but his breathing had become regular and his pulse beat stronger.

"Just tuckered out," Hatfield diagnosed the case. "Sleeping now. He'll wake up in a little and be okay."

The Mexican was, in fact, stirring before the coffee had boiled. Abruptly he opened wide, bewildered eyes and stared about him. Stark terror filmed the eyes as they rested on the tall form of the Ranger. Hatfield's quick glance caught the expression of fear, and he smiled.

"Take it easy, *amigo*," he said, "you're all right now. Just a minute and I'll have something hot for you to get inside you. That'll fix you up pronto."

The little man stared at him dazedly and Hatfield repeated the words in fluent Spanish. The Mexican found his tongue.

"Gracias, señor, gracias!" he exclaimed. "The English I understand eet," he added, a trifle proudly. "Eet I speak also, but not well."

"Fine!" Hatfield nodded, "but don't try any talking in either lingo just yet. Here, surround this cup of coffee while I cook us up some supper. I've got some ham and eggs in this saddlebag, if the eggs aren't smashed up. No, they're still in one piece. The hen that laid 'em did a good job on the shells. Hope the insides are as good. Uh-huh, they look fine," he added as he broke the eggs into the frying pan.

Jim Hatfield, usually a very silent individual, knew that nothing was more effective in putting a frightened man at his ease than just such rambling small talk. A few minutes later the little Mexican was sitting up, eating hungrily.

"Now, I wonder," the Ranger mused, studying the other while he ate. "I wonder just what he was doing out there in the desert, carrying a Government rifle? I'd better find out about that rifle, if I can."

He had already found that the gun was unloaded and that the Mexican had no ammunition in his possession.

He rolled a cigarette with the slim fingers of one hand, passed it to the Mexican and rolled another for himself. The smokes were almost consumed when Hatfield offered a casual comment and an equally casual question.

"Nice looking gun you have there, *amigo*. Where'd you happen to get it?"

Again the beady eyes filmed over. The dark face contorted.

"I—I f-found it, señor."

The voice that mumbled the words was a thick stutter. The little man's thin fingers balled into nervous fists, straightened, worked convulsively.

Hatfield, whose steady gaze missed nothing, spoke again in the same casual manner.

"You're lucky. I've always wanted a gun like that. What say you sell it to me? How much?"

Sweat beaded the Mexican's haggard cheeks and Hatfield could see the palms of his hands grow moist.

"I—I would rather not sell it, señor." He spoke little above a whisper.

"Aw, come on," Hatfield replied jovially, apparently taking no note of the other's agitation, "I'll give you a good price. More than you'll get from anybody else."

He poised a gold piece temptingly on his forefinger as he spoke.

The Mexican shook his head vehemently, although his eyes glowed at sight of the gold.

"I—I can—I—I will not sell, señor. I too have long wished for an *escopeta* like this one."

Hatfield nodded with well feigned regret.

"Okay. If you won't, you won't," he resigned himself. "Well, I'd better take these pans down to the creek and scrub 'em up a bit. Back in a minute."

He picked up the tin plates and the cups and sauntered to the bank of the little stream which flowed through the canyon. It was just within the range of the firelight, less than a dozen paces distant. As he scoured the plates with sand, he pondered the Mexican's reaction to his questioning.

"Started to say *'cannot'* instead of '*will not* sell'," he mused as he bent over the water. "That is funny. Seems like that gun doesn't belong to him, even from the *finding's keeping's* angle. Looks like he's scared of letting it get away from him. He wanted that twenty dollars, and wanted it bad. I could see it in his eyes. More money than the poor devil ever saw before, chances are. Something that looked bigger than the twenty dollars kept him from taking it, and the only thing what would look bigger is something he's scared to death of. Now what could *that* be? Nice combination—scared Mex and a brand new Government rifle. There isn't an army post within fifty miles of here, and I can't figure where else a gun like that one would come from. I suppose I ought to hang onto this fellow, but how am I going to do it and do the job I come up here to do? It'd be a dead give-away. I—"

A sudden clatter of loose stones brought his head

around with a jerk. He caught a fleeting glimpse of a dark figure vanishing from the circle of firelight. By the time he had straightened up, not even the whisper of the rope sandais could be heard above the beat of the rain. A glance told him that the rifle also had vanished.

Hatfield grinned a trifle ruefully, but with a distinct sense of relief.

"Running like a scared rabbit," he chuckled, "and there's no chance of catching him in the rain and the dark. There won't be any tracks to follow by dawn, the way the water's coming down.

"Well, that solves the problem. I didn't want to let him go without finding out something about where he got that gun, but doing that was liable to ball things up for me. We'll just forget him for a while."

He would never forget the little Mexican's face, however, nor the mysterious rifle. The big Ranger was just putting both into the back of his mind, to make room for more pressing matters.

Back beside the fire, in the shelter of the cliff, he smoked thoughtfully. The rain ceased as abruptly as it had begun and the wind died down. Soon a watery moon peeped through the clouds and cast a wan light over the wild landscape. Hatfield glanced about speculatively, nodded and got to his feet.

The sorrel horse came at his whistle and Hatfield saddled up.

"We'll just mosey on a spell," he told the horse. "According to directions, three or four more hours ought to bring us to where we're heading for. Then we'll take a good rest after we look things over and find out what's what. Okay by you?"

Goldy nodded his head and sneezed. Hatfield chuckled as he slipped the bit between the sorrel's teeth.

"Don't go trying to tell me you're catching cold," he bantered. "Fact is, I believe you're too darn slow to even catch that, you spavined old mud turtle."

Goldy's answer to this outrageous slander was an indignant snort and an apparently vicious snap at his tall master's high bridged nose. Hatfield swore at him affectionately and swung into the saddle.

East by north he rode in the pale moonlight. Less than four hours later the sorrel was daintily picking his way along the crest of a long ridge. The southern slope of the ridge was gentle, but the northern side dropped sharply toward the floor of what appeared to be a wide box canyon cutting the hills from east to west.

"This ought to be it," Hatfield mused, glancing keenly about him. "The Huachuca Trail cuts this hogback somewhere ahead, according to what those two fellows said, and right across from the notch is where *he* is. Huh! that looks like the notch down past those white rocks."

A few minutes later he reached the lip of the notch and glanced into the shadowy depths. The sides of the gash were almost sheer, the trail a score or more feet below the crest of the ridge. Where it dipped sharply down the northern slope of the ridge, it was bathed in the pale moonlight. Hatfield stiffened as he glanced in that direction.

Down the winding trail moved a long string of loaded pack mules, with mounted men beside and behind them. Just in time the Ranger caught the warning glint of quickly shifted metal. He was going out of the saddle when the rifle cracked. He heard the bullet scream through the space his body had occupied a second before. The rifle blazed a second time.

An instant later Jim Hatfield's limp body was sliding and rolling down the steep side of the notch. It thudded onto the hard surface of the trail, quivered convulsively for a moment and still. In the dark depths of the canyon, fast hoofs thudded, swiftly dying to a mere whisper of sound and ceasing altogether.

The moon slid farther toward the west, poured questing beams into the notch. They crept along inch by inch until they rested upon the Ranger's blood-streaked face, crept on and left the motionless form to the silent dark.

On the lip of the notch, the tall sorrel horse whinnied dejectedly, pawed the earth with a dainty hoof and stared downward with great questioning eyes.

Chapter IV

THE sun was rising in the east and the western peaks were crowned with pale light when Jim Hatfield groaned, groped about him with uncertain hands and opened his eyes. A white stab of pain caused him to close them quickly and for some minutes he lay fighting a deadly nausea before he dared try it again. The light had strengthened greatly by then and he could make out the crumbling sides of the notch.

A small stone tumbled down and thumped in the dust beside him. He glanced up and saw Goldy outlined hugely against the brightening sky. Painfully he sat up, raised a trembling hand to his head and felt the lump he found there. There also was a slight cut just above one cheek bone and his face was stiff with crusted blood. Somewhat shakily he got to his feet and stood swaying uncertainly for a moment.

As strength returned, he recalled the events of the night before.

His last conscious recollection had been of his boot heels skidding on a smooth stone as he had hurled himself from the saddle.

"Hit my head on the rock as I came down. Knocked myself out and rolled over the edge of the notch," he growled. "Lucky I didn't break my neck on the way down! Gosh, I feel as though I'd been pulled through a knot hole and hung up to dry!"

He was stiff and sore in every joint and his head ached abominably, but he had apparently suffered no serious injury. A few minutes later he scrambled up the side of the notch and reached his worried horse.

"This is turning out to be some trip!" he told the sorrel. "Who do you suppose those men were who started throwing lead the minute they set eyes on us? Smugglers, the chances are—those mules were all loaded and they were heading up the Huachuca from the south, like they might have come from the other side the Line.

"Funny looking loads they were carrying—long wooden boxes. Certainly weren't rawhide *aparejos,* the kind of pack sacks the Mexicans generally use. Couldn't have been silver *dobe* dollars they were packin'."

He considered a moment before he made an impatient gesture with one hand.

"I've got to put them off until later, too," he said. "Right now I've got other things to look after. But I'd like to even up for this busted head with that gun slinging gent, but it'll have to wait."

His head felt better as he turned the sorrel's nose to the north and rode down the steep slope. Soon he reached the floor of the canyon, glanced about keenly and rode slowly toward a low cliff with a decided overhang. In the shadow of the rock he dismounted, and approached the cliff.

The ground at its base was thickly grown with grass and prickly pear. High on a single stem, a cluster of drooping white yucca blossoms swayed in the breeze. To right and left, tall tree trunks, widely spaced, soared up like the columns of some great cathedral.

And here indeed was Death's cathedral. Something shone whitely beneath the green of the prickly pear. It was a skull, topping a skeleton which lay among the tatters of rotting clothes.

For long minutes Jim Hatfield stood staring down at

the skeleton. Silently he removed his wide hat and bared his dark head.

The gray eyes were somber now, and as he stared at the holes in the bullet battered skull, they turned cold as the shimmer of snow-dusted ice under a gray and wintry sky. The lean face grew bleak and the good humored mouth tightened to a thin, merciless line.

Jim Hatfield was looking down at the pitiful remains of a Ranger slain—slain in the performance of his duty.

He recalled the day, less than a week before, when two weather-beaten miners had walked into Ranger headquarters at Franklin and handed a silver star set on a silver circle to Captain McDowell. Patiently, they had answered the Captain's questions, describing in painstaking detail the location of the skeleton they had stumbled upon at the base of the cliff.

"Haid was shot fulla holes," Bill, the taller one, had said. "Rifle right beside him, bones of one hand still over it. Nope, we didn't touch nothin'—didn't see nothin' of his outfit, if he had one. Shine of his badge caught Curt's eye and that's how we knowed what he was.

"Callated we'd oughta mosey over here and tell you fellers 'bout it. Somethin' oughta be done, we figgered. Decent fellers like us don't favor Rangers gettin' blowed out from under their hats that-a-way. Nope, we didn't go tell the sheriff. We had a ruckus with him over to Helidoro, the new minin' town, and he told us to get out and not come back. Curt and me

55

was scairt he might do somethin' to make trouble for us if we come tellin' him 'bout findin' a murdered Ranger, so we decided to come over here."

Cap. McDowell thanked the miners warmly and shook hands with both. Bill and Curt had partially cleared up a mystery which had puzzled two Ranger posts for many months.

When the stern old commander, the man who "would charge hell with a bucket of water," turned to Jim Hatfield, there were tears in his eyes. Cap. Bill loved his "boys" as a father loves his sons.

"It can't be anybody but Ed Shafter," the Captain said. "Poor Ed! He was with me for a couple of years when I was stationed in the panhandle. I brought him up in the Rangers. Later he was transferred to Brooks' company. You recollect Brooks sent him to San Rosita about a year back to look into the killing of young Dick Webb by Cartina, the bandit. Was there about a week and talked to a lot of fellows; then all of a sudden he disappeared.

"Nobody knew what had become of him and nobody has seen hide nor hair of him since. Last seen of him he was in a saloon one night, talking with a little fellow who might have been an Indian. Barkeep happened to remember it, but didn't recall much what the Indian looked like. All Indians look alike to him, he said. Now these two men drop in and bring a Ranger's star they took off a skeleton, 'way up by the Huachuca Trail. Couldn't be anybody but Shafter. But what in blazes was he doing in the Tamarra Hills?"

"Must have had reasons to be there," Jim Hatfield replied quietly as he stood up. "That territory is in our district now, isn't it?"

"Uh-huh," the Captain replied, "now that we're over here at this new post. Used to be in Brooks', but it isn't any more."

"Any assignment for me, sir?" Hatfield asked. He had just arrived at the post after satisfactorily completing a difficult and dangerous mission.

"Nothing particular right now, Jim," the Captain answered.

Hatfield stretched his long arms above his head and the powerful muscles caused the seams of his coat sleeve to start. The tips of his fingers nearly reached the ceiling.

"Well, sir, guess I'd better be riding over to the Tamarra Hills for a spell, then," he stated.

"But good gosh, Jim!" the Captain remonstrated, "it's nearly a hundred miles over there and you've just come in from a mighty hard trip."

Jim Hatfield smiled down at the old Captain from his great height.

"Ed Shafter went on a longer trip, and he didn't come back," he said softly. "Ed won't rest over easy up there in the hills so long as the man that killed him is running around loose. You see, sir, I knew Shafter, too. I met him while I was running Brooks' company last year when Brooks was sick. I've got a personal interest in this business, too. Besides, the fellow who got young Dick Webb hasn't been brought in. Brooks figured it to be Cartina, and Cartina is still operating in that section, according to last reports. I've a notion that he's liable to hang around that new mining town, Helidoro. Ought to be some fat pickings for his kind there. I'll just ride up and look the situation over, if it's agreeable with you, sir."

For several minutes Captain McDowell sat staring straight ahead, his blue eyes frostier than usual.

"Jim," he said softly at length, "Rangers aren't over welcome in the Tamarra Valley, it appears. You know the Presidio post was abandoned a few months back and Brooks' outfit moved back east."

"You mean to say I can't go up there, sir?"

"I mean to say I can't *order* you up there. The Big Boss of that district seems to think local authorities can take care of things there without any outside help, and he's got enough drag at the Capital to make folks *there* think his way."

"Folks in the Tamarra Valley think that way, too?"

McDowell shook his head.

"No," he replied, "they don't. There's been more than one letter sent to headquarters asking for Ranger help to wipe out Cartina and his kind, but headquarters replied that reports of conditions were exaggerated and that the local authorities were able to cope with the situation, leaving the Rangers free for duty in districts where they were needed more. It appears John Chadwick has organized a vigilante committee to help look after things. Chadwick's paying the expenses of the organization and everything's under control, according to reports—from Chadwick."

"And Chadwick's going to run for governor."

"Uh-huh, and it looks like he'll get the nomination, and that means election, of course."

"And that means he'll run the whole state like he runs the Tamarra Valley and the county and all the counties surrounding Tamarra. Why, sir, he's running a big section of the state now! And he isn't running it the Texas way, either. It isn't right!"

"No, it isn't," Captain Bill agreed, "but it doesn't look like there's much anybody can do about it. Chadwick is honest, everybody agrees on that. He just wants things run his way. He plans on being governor, all right, and United States senator after that, I reckon, and that'll put him before the whole country, and nobody knows where he'll stop! Well, I don't suppose there's anything *we* can do about it. Fellows like Cartina are more our style."

Hatfield nodded. "Guess that's right, sir. Well, so long as you don't tell me *not* to, I guess I'll take a little ride. Maybe I'll be lucky."

The rugged old Captain said nothing, but he thrust a gnarled hand across the table to meet Hatfield's steely grip.

"Lucky!" Captain Bill growled to himself when the door had closed on his tall Lieutenant. "Lucky! Some folks may call it luck, but I have another name for it. I have a notion it's going to be almighty unlucky for the men that did for Shafter and Webb, now they have the Lone Wolf on their trail.

"Uh-huh, old Carney surely named that big fellow right. He's one fine Ranger when he's with a troop, but when he's by himself, he's a holy terror. Has never failed to outsmart or outshoot any tough, clever man he's been sent after, and he always brings his man in—or buries him! The Lone Wolf!"

Chapter V

JIM HATFIELD was thinking of that parting handshake as he stared down at the bleached bones of Ranger Ed Shafter. Stern old Cap. Bill's confidence meant a great deal to the Lone Wolf. He was thinking of that when he knelt beside the skeleton and began to painstakingly examine the bones and the rags of clothing which covered them.

The bullet riddled skull received his first attention and as he gazed at the holes in the forehead, the concentration furrow between his level black brows deepened. He recalled a paragraph in the report relative to the killing of young Dick Webb, a paragraph dealing with the bullet wounds in the Ranger's body.

"Begins to look as though the man who killed Shafter was the same one that got Webb," he muttered. "Well, that's something to go on—not much, but something. Fellows who carry guns that way aren't so common. I don't recall ever knowing more than one or two who did, and they were both lefthanded. Seems lefthanded fellows handle guns better that way; some of them, anyhow. And *that's* something to remember."

Hatfield next turned to the remnants of clothing. From the pockets he turned out a miscellany of articles—a knife, a stoppered bottle filled with matches, a pencil stub, and other trinkets. There was a notebook, but the writing on the mouldy pages was smeared and illegible.

A heavy Colt was rusted in its mildewed sheath, each chamber loaded with unfired shells. The cartridges in the belt loops were green with verdegris. Finally, from the side pocket of the coat, the one which remained entire, he drew forth three fragments of stone. With narrowed eyes he stared at them and his lips pursed in a soundless whistle. Jim Hatfield knew silver ore when he saw it and the richness of the specimens astounded him.

"I don't know what Ed was doing, 'way up here, but he sure hit on *something* worth while, judging from the looks of these rocks," he told himself.

Sitting back on his heels, he stared about him, and his keen eyes saw what the two miners, Bill and Curt, had missed.

Snugged down under the overhang of the rock, almost obscured from view by the trailing prickly pear, was a bulky object. A moment later he hauled Ed Shafter's pack into the sunlight. A quick survey of its contents deepened the line between his brows.

"Prospector's outfit!" he muttered. "Now why *that?* Was Ed on the trail of something and using this outfit to cover up with, or was he really on a prospecting trip? Funny thing for a Ranger on assignment to be doing, but you never can tell. Ed was a mining man before he joined up with the Rangers, and when a mining man gets a lead to something like the story these rocks tell, he's pretty hard to hold.

"Brooks figured it was Cartina who got Webb, and figuring that way, Ed's only job was to drop his loop on Cartina. Maybe he had a tip about when Cartina would come back on this side the Line and while he was waiting, he might have heard of something good up here in the hills. That would account for him mavericking up here with a prospecting outfit.

"And if Brooks figured right on Webb's killing, and it was Cartina did the job, Ed must have tangled with Cartina up here. Cartina might have come up here over the Huachuca Trail for some reason or other and met up with Ed. Then again Ed might have got a tip on him and was up here on that tip. All of which doesn't tie up very satisfactorily, I'll admit."

Hatfield was, in fact, evolving another theory. He was still working on it when he left the skeleton and the pack and began ranging the neighborhood of the cliff. Working away from it in widening circles he discovered, more than a hundred yards distant from its foot and on the crest of a little rise, the skeleton of a burro. The skull was drilled with a clean hole. Hatfield stood over it thoughtfully.

"Uh-huh, killed the burro, too," he immediately understood. "Didn't want it straying around and attracting attention. Begins to look more and more like the fellow who did the shooting was planning to come back to this neighborhood."

Hatfield dug a grave with Shafter's pick and shovel. He wrapped the bones in a blanket which had been protected by the waterproofed covering of the pack and gave them decent burial. Later, they could be disinterred and taken to a cemetery. He hid the pack. Then he moved off a little way, built a fire and cooked the last of his food. After breakfasting and allowing the sorrel ample time to graze, he saddled up and rode away, leaving Ed Shafter to sleep in his lonely grave.

As he left the neighborhood of the over-hanging rock, he heard, faint with distance, a deep and sullen rumble, and another, and another. He nodded understanding and headed almost due east along the slightly sloping floor of the wide gorge.

More than one angle of the mystery was puzzling Hatfield. He knew that Shafter had been a dead shot with his old single-action Colt, and could draw with blinding speed. That he had been killed by revolver shots at comparatively short range was obvious. Why had his six-gun remained unfired in its sheath, while his rifle lay beneath the clutching bones of his dead hand? And, *the rifle had been cocked when Shafter fell!* The hammer was rusted into position.

Undoubtedly Shafter had been holding the rifle when killed. Ordinarily, a man making camp would not be holding a rifle in his hands. Hatfield had no way of knowing for sure that Shafter had been making camp when killed, but the evidence pointed that way.

The pack had not yet been opened, and the Ranger had searched in vain for traces of a fire. There was no smudge against the face of the rock, the logical place for the blaze to have been kindled. A smudge there would not have been washed away, even during a period of months. Little or no rain would strike the face of the rock, no matter from what direction it came.

"Looks like he might have been watching for something, and somebody crept up on him," Hatfield deduced shrewdly. "It's funny. If he'd been shot in the back it wouldn't be so queer, but for Ed to get drilled between the eyes while facing somebody was unusual, considering the way that boy could handle a gun. Looks almost as though he knew the fellow who did it and wasn't expecting trouble from him and let him get the drop."

A mile or so distant from the rock, Hatfield became conscious of a peculiar sound drifting through the quiet of the canyon. It was a strange hissing and clicking that steadily increased in volume. It grew as he threaded his way through a grove of burr oaks and slanted around the curve of a low ridge. He passed a jutting cliff and the sound became much louder. From out the shadows rushed something huge and menacing.

Goldy gave a bound as the dark mass hurtled toward him. Hatfield was jolted sideways in the saddle and for a moment he had all he could do to control the frightened horse. The dark mass whizzed by, high

64

overhead, and almost instantly another burst from the shadows cast by the cliff. Goldy immediately had another tantrum.

"Hold it, you darned jughead!" Hatfield roared. "Those things won't hurt you!"

Goldy subsided, sweating and shivering, and still snorting his apprehension each time one of the great missiles hurtled past. The Ranger eyed them with a speculative glance that held much of approval.

"Somebody surely knows their business," he declared.

High overhead stretched two heavy wire cables. From post to post they marched up and down the gorge. From the east, where the gorge dwindled to a wide dry wash, which in turn opened upon the level rangeland, clicked an endless succession of ponderous iron buckets, empty buckets that were drawn toward the head of the gorge. But those which whizzed downward toward the rangeland were loaded to the rim with crushed stone.

"Yes, somebody surely knows their business," the Ranger repeated. "Sending the ore down from the mines by conveyor buckets. Down below are the stamp mills, where there's plenty of water and fuel. Makes all the difference in the world. The mines in this district ought to be coining money. No wonder folks say that Helidoro town is a whizzer. Things must be booming down there."

Jim Hatfield had studied engineering in the course of his two years in college, before the death of his father, subsequent to the loss of the elder Hatfield's ranch, had cut short his scholastic career. He could understand and appreciate the worth of the conveyor system working before his eyes, and admire the man who had the foresight to replace pack mules or wagons with the efficient mechanical device.

Undoubtedly the Helidoro mines were making money and making it fast. He felt surer than ever that his surmise had been correct and that the mining town would represent opportunities hard for a bandit leader like Pedro Cartina to resist. Sooner or later, he was confident, Cartina would show up in the town, either leading a raid of some sort or scouting the ground preparatory to one.

Hatfield knew that the Tamarra Valley had been Cartina's favorite hunting ground even before the mining strike. In the year and more that had passed since that sunny day when the bandit and his mysterious companion had delivered the Ranger to death by torture, Cartina had continued his depredations. For a while after Hatfield's troop had killed a number of his men and brought the Slash K trail herd back from Mexico, little had been heard of him. Later, however, Ranger reports on the district showed his renewed activity.

Hatfield, posted far to the east, had followed these reports with unflagging interest. He had looked forward to the time when he might possibly be assigned to a post that would take in the territory over which Cartina operated. The Lone Wolf had never forgotten that terrible experience on the ant hill. Later, the news of the death of young Dick Webb, apparently at the hands of the Cartina outfit, had strengthened his resolve to even the score with the snaky-eyed Mexican. The blood of a slain Ranger cried out for vengeance and Hatfield, intense in his loyalty to the outfit, would never rest easy so long as Webb's killer was not brought to justice. Now the death of Ed Shafter, Webb's successor in the district, was a further incentive to solve the mystery that brooded over the Tamarra Valley.

As to whether Cartina was responsible for Shafter's death, Hatfield was not sure. The clear-headed Ranger was not one to jump to conclusions. Many a man of the West had been killed because of his discovery of a rich mining claim. Perhaps Shafter had gone to swell their number. That he had struck it rich in the district seemed certain, to judge from the specimens in his pocket. Rich mines had been developed in the section during the past year. It looked like there might be a tie-up between those unexpected discoveries and Shafter's murder. Perhaps Cartina and his outfit must be absolved of this particular killing.

Ranger headquarters had received a number of bitter complaints from John Chadwick, the cattle king of the valley, and others. Young Dick Webb had been posted at Santa Rosita because of Cartina's continued depredations, and there had been talk of sending a troop after his death.

However, the serious outlaw trouble on the Oklahoma Border, the Cuevas county cattle war and the Comanche Raids had made it impossible to spare such a number of men. Ed Shafter, the ace man of Brooks command, had been sent to investigate Webb's death and, if possible, snare Cartina. It was all too evident now that Shafter had failed.

"Maybe he sowed the seed, though," mused the Lone Wolf as he rode along the line of the overhead conveyor. "Maybe what I've learned will be what it takes to clean up this mess."

As he turned into the shallow wash that led to where the smoke haze of Helidoro stained the clear blue of the eastern sky, Hatfield began to hear a low throb and mutter that swelled and swelled, never ceasing, never changing the steady beat of its monotonous tempo. He knew it meant stamp mills, not one but several, where the silver ore was ground to powder by the thundering dance of the ponderous steel pestles, preparatory to separating the silver from the stone.

"Sounds like big ones, too," he nodded. "Yes, this is going to be a salty town. Most anything's liable to happen, I guess."

He was not, however, prepared for what did happen as he cantered up the dusty main street just as the blue mystery of the dusk was whispering down from the hill crests.

The Ranger had already passed the gaunt buildings that housed the stamp mills before he turned into the main street of the town, which ran from north to south. Bars of light from windows and open doors were slashing the dusk with gold and in the dust of the street lay golden rectangles with misty purple edges. Men who paused before the doorways were clothed in blue and gold as light and shadow merged.

But those who suddenly came thundering down the street were not pausing anywhere. They were quirting their horses furiously, bending low in their saddles, close behind the necks of their mounts. Behind them sounded a stutter of shots and a chorus of yells.

Straight at the Ranger crashed the group of six or seven riders. Hatfield caught a glimpse of dark, savage faces and glinting black eyes. Then guns blazed and bullets stormed about him.

What it was all about, Jim Hatfield did not know, but he had a decided aversion to being shot at. A twitch of the reins and Goldy went across the street in a weaving series of jumps that made him as elusive a mark as a scared rabbit. Hatfield, knowing his trained horse would do what was expected of him, dropped the reins on the sorrel's neck and went for his guns.

With a rattling crash, both Colts let go. Fire streamed from their black muzzles, smoke wisped up before the Ranger's grim face. He swayed and weaved in the saddle, a deceptive, uncertain figure in the deepening dusk. A bullet flicked a bit of skin from his neck. Another plucked at his shirt sleeve like a ghostly hand. Again his big single actions roared.

Yells of rage and pain answered the boom of the Lone Wolf's guns. A man reeled in the saddle, gripping his smashed shoulder with reddened fingers. Another toppled sideways and thudded in the dust of the road, where he lay without sound or movement. Still another pitched forward onto his horse's neck and slithered to the ground as the group crashed past Hatfield. As they passed he saw that one was clutching the pommel to stay on his horse.

Hatfield jammed his empty guns into their sheaths and slid his rifle from the saddle boot. He flung the heavy Winchester to his shoulder and his finger crooked on the trigger. Then he hesitated, the sights of the long gun lining on the back of the rearmost rider. Without pulling trigger he lowered the rifle.

After all, he was not sure just what was going on. He had come out very much ahead in the encounter and it took a good deal of justification to shoot a man in the back. The whole business might be a case of the defeated contingent in some sort of a personal row fleeing the scene and mistaking the Ranger for an obstacle in their path.

A moment later, he was sorry he had held his fire.

Down the street came a group of men on foot, shouting, yelling, brandishing rifles and revolvers. In their lead was a tall, handsome man with iron-gray hair and flashing dark eyes. Beside him lumbered a squat individual with a tremendous spread of shoulders, a beefy face and a hard mouth. A silver star gleamed on the front of his sagging vest. In his hands he carried a heavy rifle. An instant later the muzzle of the rifle lined with Hatfield's broad breast.

"Drap that shootin' iron 'fore I plug yuh!" bellowed the sheriff. "Drap it, I say!"

Jim had no desire to argue with the forces of law and order. He did not drop the rifle, but with a slow gesture that could not be misunderstood, he shoved the weapon into the saddle boot.

"Guess that'll do just as well," he drawled, "and it won't get all full of dirt that way. Anything else you'd like me to do?"

"Yeah, get yore hands up!" snarled the sheriff. "Get his belt guns, Chadwick."

An amused light in his eyes, the Lone Wolf raised his slim hands to the height of his shoulders. The tall man moved toward him somewhat uncertainly.

"Maybe this fellow wasn't one of them, after all, Horton," he said.

"What's he doin' here with a gun in his hand, then?" growled the sheriff. "We can't take any chances, John."

"Here's two of 'em, stone dead!" a voice suddenly shouted.

Men were bending over the two riders Hatfield had downed.

"And here's nearly all of the money from the bank," another voice shouted. "Where's Elder? Let him check it and see."

The tall man had hesitated at the shouts. Now, however, he moved forward again and reached up for Hatfield's guns. As he did so a clear voice cut through the babel of whirling words like a silver knife blade of sound.

"Those guns are empty, Chadwick. You will find the bullets in the bodies of those two dead bandits there in the dust. I see our estimable sheriff is running true to form. The chances are that if he started out to arrest a card shark, he'd bring in the village padre."

Sheriff Horton whirled to face the far side of the street.

"Listen, Capistrano," he cried, "you'll horn into my affairs once too often sometime! I ain't takin' yore word for nothin'."

"It isn't necessary for you to do so," replied the silvery voice. "*Señor* Walsh here saw the whole thing also. Surely you will not contradict the president of the bank."

A thin little man came hurrying from between a couple of shacks. In his hands he carried a rifle.

"Amado's right," he said. "I was at his place when a boy ran in and yelled that the bank was being held up. We hurried over here hoping to intercept the outlaws as they rode out of town. We were too late, but we saw this man shoot it out with them and get two of them. I think he wounded one or two others. You should be thanking him, sheriff, instead of thinking of arresting him."

The sheriff sputtered and rumbled in his throat.

"Well, if that's the way of it, Walsh," he said, "we made a mistake. Yuh can't hardly blame us, though. Runnin' onto this man with a saddle gun in his hand right while we was chasin' them bandits did look sorta suspicious."

Hatfield nodded briefly, accepting the sheriff's gruff apology. He already had catalogued Horton as being a slow thinking individual with a one-track mind. Clever enough in some ways, doubtless, but liable to mistakes where quick decisions were required. And excited men, the smartest of them, are apt to jump to wrong conclusions.

In fact, he hardly heard Horton's rumbled words. His whole attention was riveted on the extraordinary individual who had shuffled from the shadows with the banker Walsh. He was hatless and a bar of light from a lighted window revealed hair like crisply curling gold. Beneath the golden hair was the most astonishingly handsome face Jim Hatfield had ever looked upon. The shapely head was set on a columnar neck that might have graced a heroic Greek statue.

But below the classic neck was pitiful distortion. There was a hump on the twisted back, another on the broad but misshapen breast. The mighty shoulders of the dwarf—he was not over five feet in height—were hunched, the arms amazingly long and powerful, ending in finely formed hands. The legs were crooked and bowed and dragged from the hips.

"Looks like God and the Devil both had a hand in making him!" the Lone Wolf exclaimed under his breath.

He was suddenly aware that the tall Chadwick was reaching up to shake his hand.

"You sure did a fine job, stranger," the big rancher congratulated. "Any time you feel like riding out to my place, I'd be mighty pleased to have a talk with you."

Hatfield had heard of the cattle baron, but had never before seen him. Chadwick was a fine figure of a man and his appearance justified the stories told about him. A light seemed to burn in the depths of his gray eyes. His jaw was heavy and powerful, his mouth firm. His nose was hooked like the beak of a hawk and more than hinted of strength and ability.

"A real fighting man who gets things done," was Hatfield's decision.

He shook hands with Chadwick and thanked him for his invitation. Walsh's voice broke in on their conversation.

"It looks like most of the money must be here," said the banker. "I can't say for sure. Where's Elder? He can tell in a minute."

"You mean the cashier?" asked a gangling cowboy. "Huh! he's daid. That tall man who rode in front shot him plumb 'tween the eyes!"

Chapter VI

MORE men were arriving on the scene. Among them was Long John Dyson, the sheriff's deputy. Horton immediately gave him instructions as to the disposal of the dead outlaws.

"I'll be expectin' yuh to show up at the coroner's inquest t'morrer, stranger," the sheriff told Hatfield. "Don't yuh be leavin' town till I give yuh permission."

Then he hurried back to the bank. Chadwick and Walsh went with him.

"Drop into the bank in the morning, I'd appreciate it," were the banker's last words to the Ranger.

Hatfield glanced down at a movement beside his horse. The hunchback was standing there, an amused gleam in his clear blue eyes.

"Invitations appear to be in order," he observed in his musical voice, "so I'll just add another one. After you have stabled your horse—Flintlock Horner runs a good stable a little ways down the next street you cross—come over to my place, *Una Golondrina*. It's on this street a little ways further on. You can't miss it. You can eat there, if you're hungry."

"I could do with about ten pounds of steak," Hatfield admitted. "I'll be there as soon as I look after old Goldy."

The hunchback nodded and vanished in the shadows. Hatfield stared after him thoughtfully. Glancing around he met the eye of a smiling young Mexican.

"Know that fellow?" he asked, jerking his thumb in the direction the hunchback had taken.

"*Si,*" replied the Mexican pleasantly. "Eet ees *Don* Amado Capistrano. He ees the very rich man. He owns the Cibola mine."

"A mining man, eh?" nodded Hatfield. "I had a notion he might be a cattleman. Legs look that way."

"*Si,*" the Mexican agreed. "*Don* Amado ees descended from those who once owned much land and many cattle. It was he who first discovered the silver in the hills. He staked the first claim and built thees town. *Si*."

Hatfield was very thoughtful as he rode slowly toward the livery stable.

"Staked the first claim," he repeated the young Mexican's words. "That's interesting. Wonder if the ore out of the Cibola is full of funny zigzag threads of silver that sort of follow the same pattern?"

The sinewy fingers of one hand dropped into a side pocket and touched the fragment of stone which rested there.

He chuckled a little later, as he passed a building whose sign proclaimed it to be "Una Golondrina."

"Una Golondrina!" said Hatfield. "That means 'one swallow' in Spanish. Must be a saloon!"

It was, and a big one. Hatfield returned to it after turning Goldy over to the care of Flintlock Horner, a six foot six individual with a pessimistic outlook on life.

"Almighty fine hoss," said Flintlock sadly, looking Goldy over with an appreciative eye. "Too fine. Chances are he'll get stole or somethin' 'fore long. That's the way things us'ally work out. He sorta reminds me of my fourth wife—no it was my fifth. She was a sorrel, too. She only had two feet, though, which made her sorta dif'rent from this cayuse. Does he kick and bite? Nope? Well, he ain't much like her after all. Yeah, I'll look after him good, don'tcha worry. I likes hosses and wimmen, and they sorta take to me, too. That's how I come to lose my sixth—wife, I mean, not hoss. Never had six hosses, 'ceptin' at one time onct."

It was early in the evening when Hatfield pushed through the swinging doors, but already the *Una Golondrina* was doing a roaring business. There was a long bar running the entire length of the room on one side. Across from the bar was a lunch counter with stools and tables. There was a dance floor, two roulette wheels, a faro bank and a number of poker tables. Threading his way through the crowd, Hatfield saw the hunchback seated by himself at a corner table. He saw the Ranger and nodded an invitation.

Hatfield sat down and the hunchback ordered a meal. The Ranger, who appreciated good food when it came his way, did ample justice to the spread. After the dishes were removed, they rolled cigarettes and sat smoking in silence. Finally the hunchback asked:

"Are you just passing through, or figuring on stopping in this district a while?"

Hatfield smoked contemplatively a moment before replying.

"Depends on whether I can find a job in this section," he said. "I'm not particular, one way or another. I've got to stay around for the coroner's inquest tomorrow. After that I'm sort of uncertain about just what I'll do. I'll have to drop my loop on a job of some kind before long. There ought to be something for a hand on one of these big spreads hereabouts. This is just about the finest stretch of rangeland I've seen for a long time. Folks are mighty lucky to own land in this section."

A cloud seemed to drift across the hunchback's clear eyes; the deep blue turned to a smoky gray. His delicately formed lips straightened to a hard line and the strong chin thrust out grimly. Hatfield saw the slim powerful hands ball into iron-hard fists. But when he spoke, his voice was unchanged in its bell-like quality and as softly modulated as before.

"Yes," he said, "it is a wonderful country and people living here are indeed fortunate. The very best of the land is owned by John Chadwick, but there are other fine ranches. I own a small one myself, adjoining Chadwick's property and bordering on the river. I acquired it recently from the widow of a man who died."

He was silent for a moment, and gradually his eyes changed color again and the hard lines of his mouth straightened out. He smiled suddenly at the tall Ranger and his teeth flashed. Again he spoke, almost diffidently.

"I was planning on offering you a job," he said. "I can use a hand or two on my little ranch, but that is not what I really had in mind. Would you consider a job other than cow punching?"

Hatfield considered a moment, his mind working swiftly.

"Depends on what it happens to be," he said at length. "I'm not much on working indoors if I can get out of it, but I'll take anything if I have to, particularly if the pay happens to be good."

"What I have to offer will pay you better than range riding, and it is not apt to keep you inside much," replied Amado Capistrano earnestly. "Ranching is but a side issue with me—as yet. My chief interest lies in my silver mine, the Cibola."

"Looks to me like you've got a *gold* mine right here," interpolated Hatfield, nodding toward the crowded bar and busy tables.

Amado Capistrano shrugged with Latin expressiveness.

"Yes, the place makes money," he admitted. "I set it up after I saw the kind of dens the silver strike brought to life. I decided there should be at least one place in the town where my workers would not be robbed. The drinks sold here are good and the games are straight."

Hatfield's keen gaze had been studying the crowd for some time.

"Some of those fellows don't look exactly like miners or waddies to me," he remarked. The hunchback smiled a somewhat wry smile.

"No," he admitted, "they don't. In fact, they are neither one nor the other. It may seem strange, but the worst element was also attracted to a place where they could get good liquor and depend on a straight game. I think I am safe in hazarding the guess that a good many of the shady characters from the Tamarra Hills and from the other side of the river are here tonight, and most every other night."

"It's likely," Hatfield replied. "You see, those fellows risk their lives, as a rule, for the pesos they manage to get their hands on. Naturally, they don't want to have it taken away from them by a crooked wheel or an extra smooth dealer, or to shell it out for drinks that are a mixture of cactus juice, rattlesnake poison and barbed wire."

"Their choice has caused me more than a little embarrassment," Capistrano said. "But to get back to the matter we were discussing. As I stated, my chief interest is my mine. The Cibola is a rich claim and much of the ore is high-grade stuff. Not only is it rich in silver but the gold content is high. It doesn't take much of that high-grade to mount into real money. Which brings me to the point. *"Señor—"* He glanced at the Ranger questioningly.

Hatfield supplied his name, giving his real one, as he did not have much fear of it being recognized. It was not an uncommon one throughout the Southwest, and he was comparatively new to the district.

"Señor Hatfield," Capistrano continued, "I am being robbed; steadily, systematically and successfully robbed. High-grade ore is vanishing from my mine at an alarming rate. The veins are as rich as ever, but the cleanup at the mills has been steadily falling off. In some manner the rich ore is being pilfered from the mine and almost worthless rock put in its place."

"What makes you think the stealing is going on at the mine?" Hatfield asked. "Maybe somebody is taking it out of the conveyor buckets on the way to the mills."

Capistrano shook his head in a decided manner.

"It isn't possible," he explained. "The number of buckets that leave the mine must check with the number received at the mill. The buckets do not pause on their trip from the mine to the mill. If they did so, it would be instantly known. Once they leave the mine they must keep on moving until they reach the mill. Even were it possible to empty them on the way down, the arrival of empty buckets at the mill would at once be noticed. No, the conveyor system is practically proof against theft. The robbing is done either at the mine or at the mill. The mill seems out of the question, so it must be the mine."

Hatfield nodded, gazing expectantly at the other. He offered no further comment. Capistrano rolled a cigarette with his tapering fingers, lighted it and inhaled a lungful of smoke. Hatfield waited patiently.

"I've tried in various ways to run the thieves down," the hunchback continued, "but as yet with no success. Complaints to the sheriff are useless—he is not overly fond of me—and my foremen and superintendents are thoroughly baffled. I watched you have that brush with Cartina and his men tonight, and I—"

"Just a minute," Hatfield interrupted. "How do you know that was the Cartina outfit?"

"The tall, black-eyed man with the lank hair, the one who rode in front, was Pedro Cartina," the hunchback replied quietly.

Hatfield nodded. Capistrano spoke again.

"Before I offer you a job," he said, "I am going to proffer some good advice—leave this district, now, tonight. Get on your horse and ride—any direction, just so it is away from the Tamarra Valley. Cartina never forgives, and he never forgets. He will avenge the killing of his men, and his vengeance is something to make the bravest shudder. You will not be safe a moment while you are here. He has followers everywhere. I would not be the least surprised if some are in this room at the moment. Cartina has power."

Again Hatfield nodded.

"He sort of wobbled in his saddle when I was cutting down on the gang," he remarked irrelevantly.

"He's hard to kill," replied Capistrano with instant understanding. "If you wounded him, that will just make his vengeance the more certain and the more terrible. I repeat, *señor,* ride, and at once."

"Thanks for the advice," Hatfield said quietly, "I'm not taking it."

The hunchback smiled.

"I did not think you would," he admitted, "but I felt it my duty to warn you. Well, if you are going to stay in the district, I'll make my offer. As I said, when I saw you in action tonight it came to me that I was watching the man who could handle the situation here if anybody could. If you'll take the job, I'll hire you to run down the thieves who are robbing me. I'll pay double what you could get on a ranch, and if you are successful, there'll be a substantial bonus for you."

"And what do I get if I'm not successful?" Hatfield asked with the suspicion of a smile quirking the corners of his stern mouth.

Amado Capistrano did not smile and there was no jest in his voice when he replied:

"The chances are, a six foot pine box!"

"That would be rather close quarters," Hatfield grinned. "I'm six-foot-four. I'll take the job!"

Chapter VII

CAPISTRANO summoned a waiter and the latter brought him pen, ink and paper. He wrote steadily for a moment or two, and as he wrote, the Lone Wolf watched him with slightly narrowed eyes and a deepening of the concentration furrow between his black brows.

"Here," Capistrano said, handing him the note, "this will introduce you to Bowers, my superintendent at the mine, and to Fuentes at the mill. They will cooperate with you to the fullest extent. You have freedom to act as you see fit."

"Let me be the one to tell these two fellows about our agreement," suggested Hatfield.

Capistrano nodded.

"I have the fullest confidence in Bowers and Fuentes," he replied, "but I will follow your suggestion. Now let's have a drink to seal the bargain."

The glasses were filled and they were just raising them to their lips when the swinging doors crashed open and a man strode into the room. It was John Chadwick and he was in a furious temper.

The uproar hushed as the tall cattle king glared

about the room, his flashing eyes finally fixing on Amado Capistrano. Lips drawn back from his teeth, he headed for the table at which the hunchback sat. Men and women made way for him, but Chadwick did not appear to notice them. At the table he halted, his face working with anger.

"Capistrano," he barked, "there was another raid on my ranch this afternoon. Two of my men killed and a couple of hundred head of cattle widelooped. And they went across your spread!"

The hunchback gazed calmly into Chadwick's blazing eyes. In his silvery voice he spoke one word.

"Well?"

Chadwick fairly choked with rage.

"Well!" he mimicked, his voice hoarse with passion. "Well, I've stood about all I'm going to stand, that's what. Those thieving killers cut across your spread and into greaserland. Then when my men started after them, your paid cutthroats held them up at your fence and wouldn't let them go through!"

"What proof have you that the rustlers went across my land?" Capistrano asked calmly.

"Proof!" sputtered Chadwick, "Proof! What other way could they go? What other way *would* they go except by Huachuca Trail? And it runs across your spread, doesn't it?"

"Then you are just surmising they crossed my land? You really do not know?"

"I know this much!" raged Chadwick. "I know one greaser always stands up for another!"

Even Jim Hatfield was not prepared for the speed with which the apparently awkward hunchback moved. Capistrano's amazingly long arms shot across the table, his slim hands gripped Chadwick's elbows. One mighty heave of his great shoulders and the ranch owner hurtled through the air. He landed on his back with a crash a dozen feet distant, rolled over, writhed for an instant and surged erect, right hand flashing to his left armpit. "Hold it!"

John Chadwick tensed rigid, the butt of the half-drawn gun gripped in his hand, the long barrel still in the shoulder holster. Face working with anger, he glared at the tall Ranger.

Jim Hatfield's hands had moved with blinding speed, sliding his big Colts from their carefully worked and oiled cut-out holsters in a blurred flicker of motion. The black muzzles yawned toward Chadwick. The Lone Wolf's voice smashed at him.

"Cut your wolf loose in the right way, Chadwick, and it's okay, but this fellow isn't heeled—you can see that. It isn't just the correct thing to throw down on a man who isn't carrying a gun."

Slowly Chadwick let the gun slide back into its sheath. His contorted features smoothed out. He nodded agreement.

"Right," he said. "You've got a head on your shoulders, stranger, but maybe if you'd just been pitched clean through yourself and out the other side, you'd be sort of off balance, too. As for you, Capistrano—"

Crash!

Just in time Jim Hatfield had caught the flicker of steel across the room. He fired over his right arm with his left-hand gun and a man reeled back against the bar, clutching a blood spouting shoulder. The gun he had furtively drawn clattered to the floor. Hatfield peered through the wisping smoke, sweeping the crowd with his cold eyes.

Outside sounded the thud of running feet. The swinging doors crashed open and men boiled into the room—lean, capable appearing men, a half dozen of them. Hatfield tensed, the big Colts clamped rigidly against his sinewy thighs. The tight group paused just inside the door, hands hovering over their gun butts, eyes sweeping the room.

One, a rangy, rawboned individual with a drooping moustache, took a long stride forward, his eyes fixed on John Chadwick.

"Yuh all right, Boss?" he called. "We heerd shootin'."

"All right, Edwards," Chadwick called back. "Just a little misunderstanding."

The lanky Edwards, Chadwick's foreman, glanced suspiciously at Jim Hatfield, who had holstered his guns and was lounging easily against the table.

"That big feller shot Bill Thompson, Ed," a voice shouted.

Edwards stiffened, but Chadwick's voice cut at him.

"Bill had it coming," the ranch owner said, "he's always going off half cocked. He meant all right but he used bad judgment."

"Shore 'pears he did," grunted Edwards, turning and striding toward the group that had laid the wounded man on a table and were attending to his injury.

"He ain't hurt bad," somebody offered. "High up through the shoulder. Didn't bust the bone."

Chadwick addressed the hunchback.

"I apologize for calling you a greaser, Capistrano," he said in a level tone. "That was out of turn and I shouldn't have done it. But that's the only thing I'm taking back," he added, his voice hardening, "and I'm warning you—the next time my men start across your spread they're *going* across. They're not going to be stopped!"

"When they have a legitimate reason for crossing, they are welcome to do so," the hunchback replied quietly, "but I don't intend to have another barn burned nor another water hole poisoned."

Chadwick glared at him, his gray eyes flashing. Then he strode straight across the room and out the door. His men, two of them supporting the wounded Thompson, followed.

Hatfield and the hunchback sat down to their unfinished drink. Business in the saloon went on as usual. The roulette wheels spun merrily, cards slithered, dice rattled. The bartenders sloshed drinks into glasses. The orchestra blared out a rollicking tune; boots thumped and dainty French heels clicked. Somebody began bellowing a song.

Capistrano leaned forward and smiled into the Ranger's eyes.

"Relative to what I said a few moments ago about your leaving this section," he said, "I now repeat the warning, more earnestly than ever. Leave Helidoro at once, tonight!"

Hatfield stared at him in astonishment.

"I thought we'd settled that," he remarked. Capistrano smiled again.

"That was before the little incident which just occurred," he said. "That was before you made an enemy a thousand times more dangerous than Pedro Cartina could ever be. You bitterly offended the most powerful man in the Tamarra Valley, one of the most powerful in the entire state, in fact. John Chadwick will never forget what you did tonight."

"Chadwick doesn't strike me as the sort who would play the game the Cartina way," Hatfield remarked.

"Oh, no, nothing so crude as that," Capistrano shrugged with Latin expressiveness. "Chadwick's methods are more subtle, but just as deadly. It is strange, but men who offend or thwart him seem to have much bad luck. Some suffer unexplainable accidents, due, apparently, to natural causes. Others are convicted of surprising crimes and are now serving long terms in the state prison. Others, wealthy and influential, suffer disastrous business reverses and become ruined men. Strange, but true."

"Chadwick has always had a good reputation, as far as I ever heard," the Ranger said. Capistrano shrugged again.

"Excellent," he admitted. "He always stays within

the law. But a smart man with great wealth and great influence can sometimes find the law remarkably elastic. Oh, yes, John Chadwick is a good citizen. No one could be more industrious in the running down of such petty outlaws as Alfredo Zorrilla and El Zopilote and others of their ilk. Crooked gamblers, gunmen, robbers and such on this side the Line have also felt the weight of his hand. John Chadwick upholds the Law. John Chadwick, in fact, *is* the Law!"

"You don't seem in awe of him," Hatfield commented dryly.

Capistrano shrugged depreciatingly.

"Chadwick hates me," he replied. "I do not agree with his notions as to how a district, or a state, should be governed. That is enough to earn his dislike. Then not long ago I managed to acquire a piece of property he had his heart set on. Also, I am a candidate for the office of sheriff, on a platform somewhat opposed to that on which his friend, Sheriff Branch Horton, is running. The election is but a short time off and Chadwick is using every means available to insure my defeat. He considers me an outlander with no right to hold office.

"Really, Señor Hatfield," he added, smiling his charming, melancholy smile, "I am forced to believe that at the bottom John Chadwick is an honest man. He truly believes what he believes. He feels that he is divinely appointed to control the destinies of his fellowmen and that anyone who opposes him should be ruthlessly crushed. It is an attitude developed and fostered by the great landowners. My ancestors, some of them at least, held much the same attitude. If they considered a thing right, it, of necessity, *must* be right because they believed it was. John Chadwick is of the same breed."

Hatfield nodded his understanding. He too had encountered this attitude on the part of the barons of the open range. Accustomed to ruling with an iron hand, they were intolerant of any interference and willing to go to desperate lengths to maintain the prerogatives they honestly believed should be theirs.

Chadwick, one of the really large owners of the state, doubtless was subject to this feeling in a marked degree and would bitterly resent anything that might be construed as an encroachment upon what he considered his rights and privileges. He surrounded himself with men of his own kind, who saw eye to eye with him and were ready at all times to uphold him.

"Those rannies of his who barged in here are a salty lot," Hatfield mused as he sipped his drink. "They're not the kind to take water from anybody and they're all set to back their boss up in anything he says. Maybe Chadwick isn't altogether a bad fellow, but he belongs to the breed that has to be taken down a peg every now and then. Can't get it through their heads that this country is for everybody and not just for a few big toads who're liable to slop all the water out of the puddle if they keep on swelling themselves up."

Flintlock Horner had a spare room over the livery stable and he rented it to Hatfield for the night. Before lying down, the Ranger sat on the edge of the little built-in bunk and smoked a final cigarette. His face was very thoughtful and there was a speculative light in his gray eyes.

He was thinking, in fact, not of the stirring events of the past twenty-four hours, but of a commonplace incident that, ordinarily, would have been of little interest. He was visioning Amado Capistrano writing that note of introduction to his mine superintendent—*writing with his left hand!*

Then he dismissed the matter with a shrug and stretched out to relax in slumber, resolutely putting puzzles out of his mind. In a moment he was asleep.

Chapter VIII

IN MEN who for long periods of time ride stirrup to stirrup with deadly danger, there develops an eerie sixth sense that ofttimes warns of approaching peril. Many a time during his adventurous years as a Ranger, Jim Hatfield had felt death's stealthy approach. Many a time this strange premonition of evil had saved him. He had learned to respect the seemingly inexplicable and to accept the warnings when they came.

Thus, when he suddenly awoke with every nerve tingling and every muscle tense, he did not dismiss the alarming manifestations as figments of an over-wrought imagination. Silent, motionless he lay, ready for instant action, listening with keen ears, endeavoring to pierce the quiet dark of the little room.

From the other side of town came the monotonous rumble of the stamp mills. In the livery stable below a horse pawed impatiently. Another stamped in his stall. A strain of music drifted faintly from some still active dance hall. Otherwise the night was silent.

And yet—the thick dark was acrawl with menace. Hatfield could feel it, a stealthy, furtive, deadly thing that drew closer and closer. Waiting there in the black shadow, the palms of his hands grew moist, his muscles ached with strain. The weird premonition fairly screamed its warning in his ears. Hollow-eyed murder was abroad in the night; was approaching the cot in the little room.

Slowly, quietly, the Ranger stretched his hands toward the heavy Colts always within easy reach. He gripped the black butts, drew the big guns from their sheaths and lithely slipped over the foot of the cot. Crouched against the end wall of the room, he watched the opaque blot that was the door.

A crack split the intense dark, a dimly luminous crack that widened by almost imperceptible degrees. A tiny creaking filtered through the silence; the glowing crack remained stationary for a long moment. Then again it began to widen, slowly, steadily as the door opened and the feeble beams from the lantern hanging in the stable below seeped through the dark.

The clean edges of the widening crack of light abruptly blurred as a grotesque shadow absorbed the glow. Jim Hatfield, tense against the wall, saw a man slip into the room. Another followed him, and another. They merged with the shadows thronging the room.

The crack of light now stretched across the room and faintly illumined the bunk built against the wall. It fell on the tumbled blankets from under which the Ranger had slipped, and in the illusive gleam the bedding took on the shape of a huddled human form. The indistinct shape was suddenly blotted out by the shadow of a man who leaned over the cot.

There was a flashing glitter, then the sodden ripping blows of a knife that slashed the blankets to ribbons. Instantly there followed a startled curse.

"Hell's fire! There ain't nobody here! He's—look out!"

With a rattling crash, both the Ranger's guns let go. The knife wielder screamed shrilly, whirled sideways and thudded to the floor. The walls of the little room seemed to reel and bulge to the roar of six-shooters.

Hatfield, pouring lead at the two shadowy figures, ducked and weaved, sliding back and forth along the wall as bullets hammered the boards. He heard another yell, snapped a shot at a fleeing shadow and hurled his body to the floor as fire streamed through the dark.

Feet were thudding on the stairs. They hit the landing just as the two remaining killers hurtled through the door. With a terrific roar, a shotgun let go. Then there was another deafening crash as a cursing, clawing, fighting knot of men whirled end-over-end down the narrow stairs.

Hatfield reached the door just as the shotgun bellowed a second time. He saw a slight, dark man literally blown across the stable, his face a bloody smear of buckshot-riddled flesh. He saw the grim, rage-distorted face of lanky Flintlock Horner glaring through the shotgun smoke, and for the briefest instant he glimpsed another face as a tall, broad-shouldered man bounded across the stable toward the outer door—just a fleeting glimpse of a weatherbeaten face with flashing black eyes and a lean, hard jaw.

For an instant he thought the fleeing man might be Pedro Cartina, but as instantly discarded the thought. The man was taller, broader, and his skin was tanned, not swarthy.

All this Hatfield noted in the split second before he lined sights on the fleeing man and pulled trigger. The hammers of his guns fell with a chilly double-click on empty cartridges.

Ejecting the empties and jamming loaded shells into one gun, he bounded down the stairs. Flintlock flung up the reloaded shotgun, but Hatfield roared a warning in the nick of time. Getting the gun down threw Horner off-balance, however, and he barged smack into the racing Ranger. The two hit the floor in a wild tangle. By the time they scrambled to their feet and shot out the door, the fleeing man was nowhere in sight.

"I told you somebody'd try to steal that yaller hoss!" bawled Flintlock. "A yaller hoss and a red-haided woman! They means trouble all the time! The only thing what's wuss'n either of 'em is both!"

The stable keeper was a sight. One eye was rapidly closing, a bleeding nose had already swelled to twice its normal proportions, and his face was otherwise scratched and battered. He held the ten-gauge shotgun at full cock and brandished it wildly. Hatfield looked into the yawning black muzzles and hastily stepped aside. Horner hammered the butt of the gun on the floor to lend emphasis to his shouts and both barrels went off with a roar like the crack of doom.

The blast reeled the startled Flintlock into a stall, and a mule promptly kicked him out again. He scrambled to his feet, rubbing the seat of his trousers, and resumed his yelling where he had left off. Hatfield got the shotgun and shoved it out of sight behind a feed barrel.

Men were pouring into the stable, aroused by the terrific tumult. They bellowed questions which nobody could answer, and for a few minutes a fair imitation of bedlam ensued. Hatfield finally restored some semblance of order, and the two bodies were hauled forth and examined.

Both wore the garb of Mexicans. The face of the man who had received the shotgun charge was little more than a bloody smear. That of the one Hatfield had shot was swarthy, slit-mouthed, high of cheek-bones and nose bridge.

"Pure-blood Yaqui," was the verdict of members of the crowd. "Coupla hoss lifters from t'other side the river, that's what."

Flintlock Horner's contention that Hatfield's splendid sorrel had been the object of the raid was accepted without argument. The Ranger expressed no opinion to the contrary.

Sheriff Horton bustled in a little later and glared at Hatfield.

"'Pears yuh been mixed up in plenty of trouble since yuh hit town," he growled accusingly.

"Meaning?" the Lone Wolf drawled.

"Meanin' nothin', 'cept watch yore step!" Horton snorted. "This is a law abidin' section and we don't favor quick-draw men hangin' out here. But don't yuh be pullin' out 'fore the coroner's inquest this mornin'."

He stamped out, grumbling under his breath. Flintlock Horner tentatively fingered his swelling nose and grunted.

"Some day, plumb by accident, Horton's gonna have a sensible thought—and it'll bust his head wide open!" said Flintlock.

After the room was put in order, Hatfield went to bed again. He could hear Horner swearing about the stable, searching for his shotgun. Hatfield chuckled as he closed his eyes, but the chuckle died and his mouth set in stern lines as he recalled the face and form of the tall man racing across the stable floor.

"Uh-huh, and it was a big, tall, broad-shouldered fellow who pegged me down on that anthill down in Mexico. I wonder, now? Could that be the brains behind Pedro Cartina?"

Chapter IX

JIM HATFIELD decided to ride to Capistrano's A Bar C ranch the following afternoon.

"It'll be better to have it look like I'm just taking a job of riding with you," he told the hunchback. "If I go spreading around as a sort of special detective you've hired to run down the men making away with your ore, they'll have the same line on me as they have on the sheriff and his deputies. There's some mighty shrewd people back of this business, and it wouldn't be wise to give them any more headway on us than we have to."

Capistrano agreed with the wisdom of this course.

"I'll ride to the ranch with you," he told the Lone Wolf. "I'll introduce you to Felipe, my foreman, and tell him that you are going to ride the west range and plan winter shelters and get a line on waterholes and feed in the canyons. Then you can cut into the hills whenever you take a notion. My spread covers all that section.

"The Huachuca Trail cuts through the hills within a few miles of the conveyor lines and not a great way west of the mines. My conveyor line is the one farthest west, incidentally. On the east are the lines of the Root Hog, the Lucky Turn, the Humboldt, and others. Yes, it is a big working. Those hills are bursting with silver, something no one ever suspected and which I discovered by merest chance. I'll tell you about it sometime."

"I'd be interested in hearing it," Hatfield admitted.

Sheriff Horton's office was also the office of the coroner, a bewhiskered and cantankerous individual known as Ol' Doc Draper. Doc was a typical cow country physician, shrewd, irascible, efficient. He was close to seventy years of age but had the energy of a man forty years younger. Hatfield immediately placed him as a character, and a likeable and dependable one. His questions were brief and to the point.

"Murdered in performance of his duty by Pedro Cartina or some other outlaw like him," was his verdict on the death of the bank cashier Elder.

"Cashed in when they had it comin'," he ruled relative to the bandits Hatfield had shot.

"Yuh shore must have almighty good eyesight to pick out that leadin' rider as Cartina," he told Amado Capistrano, a point Jim Hatfield had already noted.

That finished the inquest. Sheriff Horton, however, had a word with Jim Hatfield on his own account.

"Yuh 'pear to be the right sort," he told the Ranger, "but yuh seem to be gettin' into the wrong comp'ny. I've been told yuh've signed up to ride for Capistrano. I ain't got nothin' personal 'gainst Amado, but he don't strike me as bein' jest the right sort. The worst characters in this here district hang out in his place, and he hires mostly greasers for his mine and his spread.

"He hadn't oughta had that spread in the fust place. Lots of folks figger it was some of his outfit what did for Walt Bloodsoe, who owned A Bar C 'fore Capis-

98

trano got holt of it. He shore was all-fired quick to hustle over and buy the spread offa Walt's widdy after Walt was cashed in. John Chadwick was gonna take over the outfit, but Amado got there fust. Seems almost like he knowed to make his plans in advance. I'm jest tellin' *yuh*."

Hatfield mentioned the matter to Walsh, the bank president, to whom he had taken a strong liking.

"I don't know about that," Walsh said, "but I do know that Amado paid the Widow Bloodsoe more than the ranch was worth; more, I believe, than she could have gotten from anybody else."

Which gave the Lone Wolf something more to ponder over as he cinched Goldy and rode out to meet his new employer.

Capistrano wore regulation cow country garb, his only concession to his Spanish blood being an ornate *sombrero* heavy with silver. He wore heavy, double cartridge belts and two guns. One holster, the left, swung much lower than the other. The sheaths were cut high and only the black butts of the guns showed.

"Both regulation .45 frames, or I'm mistaken," Hatfield decided, after a quick glance. "He's not a real two-gun man but the sort of fellow who draws one gun first and then draws the other one to back it up. Pulls the left one most of the time and always first. Yes, there's no doubt about it, he's really left-handed—doesn't just write that way."

They rode in silence for the most part. Capistrano seemed busy with thoughts of his own, and the

Ranger, too, had plenty to think about. The hunch-back, likeable though he seemed, was occupying a peculiar position in the Ranger's mind. He was the first man to benefit by the silver strike, a strike that had taken place, as near as Hatfield could ascertain, at about the same time Ed Shafter had vanished into the Tamarra Hills.

The Cibola mine, while located some distance from where the slain Ranger's body had been found, was in the same general section—in the same wide gorge, to be exact, only farther east and to the north, a district it was quite logical to believe Shafter had passed over to reach the Huachuca Trail.

And Capistrano was left-handed—and the Ranger's experience had been that it was usually a left-handed man who carried guns of the type that had inflicted the death wounds of both Shafter and young Dick Webb.

Then there was the poor opinion of Capistrano held by Sheriff Horton, who, to all appearances, was an honest if somewhat stupid officer; and by John Chad-wick, easily the foremost citizen of the valley, a man who had held positions of trust and was spoken of for positions of still greater honor.

"Well," mused the Lone Wolf, "a man is innocent till he's proved guilty. But," he added, the corners of his firm mouth quirking a trifle, "that doesn't mean a man can't keep his eyes open."

The A Bar C was a comparatively small ranch, but a good one, Hatfield quickly decided. It was well wooded and a little stream flowed through it from northwest to southeast. There were also quite a number of waterholes, while to the south, the silver sheen of the Rio Grande formed its boundary. Curved about the spread, east and north, like a lion around a crouching lamb, was John Chadwick's great Circle C, the finest and by far the largest outfit in the valley. Still farther east was the Rocking Chair, the Lazy V, the Bowtie, and others.

Capistrano's half-dozen riders were young Mexican *vaqueros* with dark faces and white grins. They were courteous and pleasant. Felipe, the foreman, was jolly and moon-faced and he had an infectious chuckle. They conversed with Hatfield in broken English and many gestures. The Lone Wolf spoke Spanish fluently and understood it equally well but he did not always allow the fact to become common knowledge.

The riders treated Capistrano with great respect, addressing him as *Don* Amado.

"Their fathers and their fathers' fathers before them were retainers of my family," the hunchback explained. "The time was when more than twice a hundred men rode the great *hacienda* of the Capistranos, which included this entire valley."

He was silent for a moment gazing with eyes that seemed to dream across the wide expanse of beautiful rangeland to the far distant edge of the grim Tamarra Desert that stretched eastward from the Hueco Mountains, curving north around the Tamarra Hills and then rolling southward to the Rio Grande. The heat-tortured waste of gray alkali and sand enclosed the rich valley and the barren silver hills. The desert was sinister, but here on the green range was sunshine and peace.

"A mighty pretty country," said the Lone Wolf.

"Yes," said Amado Capistrano.

Jim Hatfield rode the range the following morning.

"I can find my way about," he told Felipe, when the foreman courteously offered to place a guide at his disposal.

"Sometimes a fellow just looking around can see what a fellow who knows the country misses," he added by way of explanation.

Felipe agreed and answered questions relative to general directions. He also offered a word of warning.

"The Huachuca Trail crosses our land near the foot of the hills," he said. "The señor will do well to beware that trail. The men who use eet are all too often, what you call eet, not nice. They are *muy malo,* very bad."

Hatfield thanked the foreman and rode away. All day he probed the canyons and gorges, drifting far to the south, until he reached the shimmering band of the river. Then he turned north by west and rode into the red eye of the setting sun. Dusk was misting over the range before he reached the foothills of the Tamarra.

It was a weird night! A cold, dead moon soared up over the dim crags beyond the desert, shining fitfully through scurrying clouds. A wailing wind swept restlessly through the burr oaks and the sage. There were patches of desert bordering the gaunt slopes of the hills and on them giant chola cactuses brandished grotesque arms that twisted and writhed like malignant devils tortured with pain. The wan moonlight cast strange shadows and all things were distorted and unreal.

Just as distorted and just as unreal was the writhing gray ribbon of the Huachuca Trail. Jim Hatfield had often sensed an intangible something about the trail that differentiated it from others.

There was something brazen about the Huachuca, something sinister, something definitely evil. It did not slip furtively, nor did it march boldly. It writhed—writhed like a bad-tempered snake that knew its power for evil and its ability to destroy.

The Huachuca slid into gloomy canyons as if it belonged there, slid out again, seeming to carry some grim secret that would be well worth the telling but which wouldn't be told, unless bleached bones could talk.

In the shadow of a grove of burr oaks, Hatfield pulled his big sorrel to a halt. For long minutes he sat gazing at the trail. Suddenly he tensed in the saddle and eyes narrowed.

Sound was drifting up from the south, from the direction of that broad, shallow river that shimmered in the furtive moonlight. At first it was but a whisper, but it grew steadily to a mutter, a faint drumming, a low thunder.

Out of the gray cloaked dark burst shadowy figures, sweeping north with steady swiftness. Hatfield identified them as mounted men. Leaning forward he clamped his hand gently over the sorrel's nose. Goldy was usually a silent horse, but he might feel an urge to call out a comradely greeting to one of the horses passing up the trail. And Hatfield much preferred his presence in the grove to remain unnoted. Instinctively he counted the riders as they passed.

He missed some, but more than a hundred had flashed by the grove before the last hoof-beat dimmed away into the distance.

"And every one carrying a rifle!" the Ranger muttered as he urged Goldy onto the trail.

Silent, watchful, he rode up the gray track in the wake of the speeding band. Intent on what was ahead, he did not see the shadowy forms that rode half a mile to his rear. Nor did this second group of riders, apparently hurrying to overtake the first, realize that the Ranger rode between them and their objective. They were a compact body, many less in number than those ahead, and their leader was a tall man whose broad brimmed hat was drawn low over his eyes.

On through the gloomy gorge burrowed the Huachuca Trail, dipping and rising, snaking along in the shadow of overhanging cliffs, turning sharply to the left at length and climbing along the face of a beetling wall of rock. To the right was a sheer drop into black darkness where water boiled and murmured. A swift stream ran along the base of the cliff, a deep little river that gushed from under a towering cliff at the head of the gorge and thundered into a

yawning chasm beneath another cliff a few miles farther to the south. It was a "lost river" of mystery that
held its course from darkness to darkness and hugged
the canyon wall as if shrinking away from the light.

Jim Hatfield, however, paid scant attention to the
bluster of the water as he rode swiftly up the
Huachuca Trail. His mind, set at trigger edge, concen-
trated fully on the grim band of armed men who rode
the trail ahead. He was certain that he had, partly by
lucky accident, intercepted Pedro Cartina and his
raiders as they rode north to rob and murder.

"Maybe I can get a line on what they're up to and
figure out some way to crack down on them before
they can get back across the Line," he muttered,
peering through the gray darkness and straining his
ears for signs of the quarry.

He knew that the valley was up in arms against the
outlaws and that he could swiftly organize a force
competent to deal with even a large and well armed
band. The recollection of the rear guard fight he and
his Rangers had waged against the Cartina outfit came
to his mind and he chuckled.

"If I can get a dozen men together, armed with good
Winchesters, we'll hang onto them and head them off
from the river," he declared. "It'll work out just like it
did that time in Mexico, only we'll round up a different kind of cattle this time."

The sky was clearing and the moon casting more
light. The trail ahead shimmered wanly as it straightened out and mounted a long rise. Hatfield rode

warily, his eyes fixed on the distant crest where the trail seemed to end abruptly. The men he followed were not in sight and he could not longer hear the sound of their horses, but there was the danger that they might be just the other side of the dip. Anxious to catch up with them, but not daring to risk topping the rise and finding himself in their midst, he slowed the sorrel to a walk and halted him a score of paces distant from the crest. He swung to the ground and crept forward on foot, bending low and hugging the cliff wall. A moment later he could see over the rise.

A half mile or so ahead was the band, riding slowly along the winding trail. They were bunched together and it seemed to the Ranger that an air of anticipation hung over the group.

"Looks like they were expecting something or somebody," he told himself.

He shifted his position slightly, moved away from the cliff in order to get a clearer view.

Cr-r-r-rack! Wham! Whe-e-e-e!

A bullet screamed past, scant inches from his head, slammed against the cliff, screeched off on a wild ricochet and whined away into the darkness. Hatfield ducked instinctively and whirled, guns coming out. The slug had come from *behind him!*

One swift glance and he was racing for his horse. Down the trail, only a few hundred yards distant, rode a body of men, thundering toward him, yelling and shooting. Hatfield reached Goldy amid a rain of bullets, swung into the saddle and yelled to the sorrel.

Goldy shot forward in a racing gallop, topped the rise and thundered down grade. A few seconds later the pursuing band swooped over the rise and bullets began to whine past the Ranger.

The group ahead had halted. Hatfield, swiftly estimating the distance, felt safe from their guns for a few minutes longer. He was astounded when a bullet from their direction fanned his face and another plucked at his sleeve.

"They've got guns that can *carry!*" he growled.

His predicament was truly desperate. Between two hostile forces, bullets storming about him, one of which would surely find its mark, to his left was an insurmountable wall of rock, to his right a sheer drop into the river. How far it was to the canyon floor Hatfield had no way of knowing. The questing beams of the moonlight did not penetrate the gloom of the gorge and the elusive murmur of the water told him little.

"Have to chance it, though," he grunted as a slug grazed his cheek. He swerved the sorrel sideways, gripped the reins with steely fingers and braced himself in the saddle.

Goldy did not want to take the jump, and wildly snorted his protest. But he took it, bunching his dainty hoofs and tensing his big body, as he shot over the lip of the cliff.

Down he rushed—down—down, the wind shrieking past in a hurricane, black fangs of rock soaring up to meet him. He grazed a reaching hand of jagged stone, struck the water with a splash and vanished under the inky surface. Hatfield swung from the saddle, gripped the sorrel's mane and held tight as they slowly rose from the dark depths. Instantly a mighty current seized horse and man and hurled them downstream— toward the point where the river roared ominously as it dashed into the bottomless chasm beneath the cliff.

On the trail above sounded the angry yells of the raiders and the crackle of their guns as they spattered the unseen water with bullets.

Hatfield paid scant attention to the whining lead. His entire effort was put forth in a desperate struggle to reach the shore before the current hurled him and his horse to certain destruction in the depths under the black cliff. It seemed to him, strong swimmer that he was, that he did not gain an inch toward the bank as they shot downstream.

A questing beam of moonlight lighted the surface ahead, and rested on what looked like an undulating snake that stretched from the cliff wall to the far bank of the river. Hatfield knew it to be the curve of the stream as it took the last terrible plunge into the underground depths. The current seemed to drag at him with hungry fingers, the river seemed to shimmer exultantly in the moonlight.

There was a scraping sound of iron on stone. Goldy snorted explosively and gave a wild scramble. The sorrel's hooves had touched bottom. He lunged for the shore. Hatfield, gripping the horse's mane with iron fingers, was dragged after him. An instant later his own boots were scraping on the rocks. Together they floundered through the shoaling water and scrambled up the shelving bank, less than a score of feet distant from the curving plunge of the river.

For a long time the Ranger lay on the coarse grass of the canyon floor. Goldy stood over him with hanging head. Both were exhausted. Finally, the Ranger summoned strength to wring the water from his clothes, empty his boots and at length swing into the saddle. He rode slowly down the gorge, cutting diagonally to the east. He chuckled grimly as he rode.

"Well, boy," he told the sorrel, "about the only thing we found out tonight is that those fellows have got guns that carry as far as ours. There won't be any more hanging back and picking them off from now on. It'll be straight fighting, man to man, and there are plenty of them to match up with the vigilante committees being rounded up in this valley. I reckon it's about time to see what brains will do."

His mind drifted back to that dark night on the Tamarra Desert, the stricken little Mexican and the new model rifle.

"That's the answer," he growled. "But how in blazes did they get Government rifles? Well, when I find out how, and who engineered the deal, I'll have a line on whoever's back of that outfit. I certainly don't believe it's Cartina."

And the chuckling Hill Gods warped still another thread into Death and Destiny's tangled web as Jim Hatfield, all unknowing, rode to meet with the man who was the "brains" of Pedro Cartina's outfit.

Chapter X

HATFIELD rode parallel to the trail until it poured through the notch. There he left it, striking across the canyon to the spot where Ed Shafter lay buried. He paused beside the lonely grave, glanced down and bared his head. High in the tops of the pines, the wind mourned and whispered. The moonlight seeped through the rents in the scurrying clouds and the whole scene was shadowy and unreal. The notch through which the Huachuca Trail entered the canyon took on the semblance of grinning fleshless jaws and the misty trail itself seemed to writhe slowly with torpid life.

The Ranger rode away from the grave and to the overhanging rock in whose shade the two miners had found the body. For long minutes he sat gazing into the gloom beneath the gnarled overhang. As he gazed he seemed to see a crouching figure there, a figure that fixed eager eyes on the gloomy notch that knifed the canyon wall, a figure tense with waiting, in its pose an expectancy. And instinctively he knew that figure to be Ed Shafter as he had crouched in the shadow of the rock nearly a year before—crouched and waited for something to take form in the dark notch which cramped the Huachuca Trail.

"Yes, that's what he was doing up here," muttered the Lone Wolf. "Ed was on the trail of something— that prospector outfit was a blind."

His eyes narrowed as he stared toward the notch and the concentration furrow between his dark brows deepened in perplexity.

"But how in blazes did he come to have a pocket full of rich silver ore?" he added.

Back and forth across the moonlit terrain his keen gaze wandered, probing, analyzing, and all the while his fertile brain grouped and catalogued the meager facts as he knew them.

"That's why he had his rifle," he deduced. "He was watching the notch and prepared for long-range shooting. But how did the killer, whoever he was, slip up behind Ed and get the drop on him? Did he know Ed was here? Was it somebody Ed trusted and maybe had working with him? I don't think anybody could see Ed down there in the dark under the overhang, particularly from the trail. Let's see, now—"

Suddenly his glance paused on the little hilltop where lay the bones of the slain burro. It shifted to the trail and back again. The gray eyes blazed with excitement.

"That's it!" he exclaimed. "That's it, certainly! The burro wandered up onto that hill and was standing there in plain sight. Somebody spotted the burro and come slipping around looking for the man who owned him. He spotted Ed, maybe when he stepped out of the shadow. Spotted him and drilled him dead center."

But the perplexity had not left his eyes as he built a tiny fire in a sheltered hollow some distance from the hanging rock and cooked a meal. He was still convinced that the man who had faced Ed Shafter that fatal night was someone the Ranger knew—knew and trusted, or at least someone he credited with no hostile intent, until too late. The cocked rifle was mute evidence that Shafter had realized his error before he died.

Still pondering, Jim Hatfield rolled into his blankets. In a few moments he was asleep.

He was up again at dawn and saddling Goldy after a scanty breakfast.

"Let's go take a look at the mine," he said as he swung himself into the saddle.

The buckets were crashing past when he reached the conveyors, and Goldy did not favor them any more than formerly. He snorted disgustedly as the Ranger turned his nose parallel with the marching line of cables.

"If we follow this, we can't help but fetch up at the mine," Hatfield assured the horse, "I know this isn't much of a trail, but you've made it over worse ones. Stop your kickin'!"

Deeper and deeper into the hills bored the twin lines of cables. Twice within the hour, Hatfield heard the dull boom and rumble of distant blasts, proof that he was approaching the mines, which were still a considerable distance off, judging from the sound.

The conveyor line was running past towering cliffs that formed the eastern wall of the gorge. The cliffs, seamed with fissures, mottled with mineral stains, shut out the sun and cast an unnatural gloom over the canyon floor. Goldy shivered in the dank shadow and snorted disapproval. He snorted again as his hoofs crunched on a litter of loose stone.

Hatfield glancing down, abruptly pulled the sorrel to a halt. The stones were not boulders worn by water and weather. Their edges were sharp and their sides showed a clean line of cleavage from some parent body.

The Ranger glanced up at the conveyor line. From time to time the loaded and empty buckets clicked past, sliding evenly past the dark loom of the cliffs. There was a curve in the line here, quite slight, but enough to cause the pulleys to whine a bit.

"Looks like some of the ore gets jostled off here," he mused as he swung down from the saddle. He watched each loaded bucket as it approached lest there be a reoccurrence of the spillage—some of the bits of ore were large enough to inflict a painful injury, falling from such a height—but the careen of the loaded conveyors was slight and no fresh stones swelled the scattering at the base of the cliff.

"Must have been an extra heavy load in one of them," the Ranger decided as he picked up several fragments of the fallen ore. Stepping back from the line of the cables, he carefully examined the bits of stone, and as he did so, his eyes turned coldly gray and his bronzed face grew bleak. Pulling a small chunk of stone from a side pocket, he compared it with the fragments he had picked up.

The peculiar zigzag pattern of the blue threads of

silver was identical. Without a doubt, the Cibola ore came from the same ledge as had the bits of weather stained rock he had found in the pocket of Ed Shafter's moldering coat!

For many minutes, Jim Hatfield stood beside the scattered fragments of ore. Overhead the conveyor buckets whined past on their humming cables. A gloomy rift in the cliff face, directly opposite, seemed to leer at him like an eyeless socket. Everything in these grim hills seemed to smack of death and decay and sly treachery. Eyes stern and brooding, the Lone Wolf mounted his golden horse and rode up the dark gorge.

Two miles farther and the hum and clatter of the mine was apparent. Abruptly the cliffs fell back and revealed a wide space flooded with sunshine as golden as the sorrel's coat. The spot appeared singularly wholesome after the sombrous gorge—like a flower garden reached by way of a narrow passage through a thick wall.

Here were the mine buildings, the mouth of the shaft which burrowed into the bowels of the earth and the cheerful voices of the workers.

Not all the voices were carefree and peaceful, however. In front of a building marked "Office" a loud altercation was taking place. Hatfield was surprised to see that one of the disputants was Sheriff Branch Horton. The other was a tall, broadshouldered man with a weatherbeaten face and flashing eyes. His mouth was hard, his jaw lean and prominent.

The sheriff, whose clothes were powdered with gray dust and who showed other evidence of a long, hard ride, was red-faced and angry. A little to one side, a group of men were watering their horses and glancing from time to time toward the bickering pair. John Chadwick, the tall cattle king, was one of the group and Hatfield recognized Edwards, his foreman, and other men who had entered the *Una Golondrina* on the night of Amado Capistrano's argument with Chadwick. Bill Thompson was there, his shoulder bandaged, but apparently little the worse for his encounter with the Ranger. All were grinning and apparently amused.

They glanced up at the sound of Goldy's hoofs and their faces hardened. Horton and his adversary were too intent on each other to notice the new arrival.

"Yuh'd do better spendin' a little time runnin' down the men who are robbin' this mine right and left 'stead of scootin' 'round in the hills chasin' a bandit who, the chances are, is south of the Rio Grande, all the time," the tall man boomed as Hatfield came within hearing.

Sheriff Horton swore a crackling oath.

"I ain't a detective, Bowers," he shouted. "I'm a peace officer and I arrest people I know has committed a crime. I'm plumb shore and sartain it's some of yore own outfit that's doin' the stealin' up here. *You* get a line on 'em—that'd oughta be part of yore bus'ness—and I'll drap a loop on 'em quick enough. I *know* what Cartina and his outfit has done and whenever I get a line on *him,* I'm gonna foller it."

"Yeah, foller, and never ketch up!" snorted the tall Bowers. "Yuh couldn't ketch cold on a rainy day!"

Horton opened his mouth to roar an answer, when he caught sight of Jim Hatfield lounging easily in his saddle. He waved a hand in greeting. The Ranger shrewdly surmised he was glad of an opportunity to change the subject and get away from the irate mine superintendent.

"Strays must be sproutin' wings, if they've took to amblin' up this high," he observed jocularly.

"I had to ride to the west range and took a notion I'd amble up and look the Boss's mine over before I rode back," Hatfield explained easily. "Nice section up this way."

"Nice for them that likes it!" grunted Horton. "I shore have had enough of it since yest'day aft'noon. Been up in these hills ever since then. Heerd tell Pedro Cartina was snoopin' 'round up here and started out with a posse to ride herd on him. Spent mosta the night freezin' under a cliff way over toward the nawtheast of Chadwick's range. John's been losin' a sight of steers of late and he's gettin' almighty tired of it."

"Been in the hills all night?" Hatfield asked in sympathetic tones, his glance running over the sheriff's posse and back to the stocky peace officer.

"Uh-huh," Horton grunted, "all night. Well, reckon we'd better be headin' back for town, now the bronks has filled up. Yuh ridin' back thataway?"

"Not just yet," Hatfield replied. The sheriff nodded.

"I'll head up this way in a day or two and see if I can

do anythin' for you, Bowers," Horton flung at the mine superintendent. Bowers grunted something unintelligible and glanced inquiringly at Hatfield.

The possemen swung into their saddles. John Chadwick favored the Ranger with a curt nod.

"That invitation to ride over to my place still holds," he said, "even though I don't think much of your choice of outfits to sign up with."

"Nobody else offered to sign me up, sir," Hatfield responded quietly, "and I haven't seen anything wrong with the one I'm with."

"You will, if you stay around long enough," the cattle king replied. "Come on Horton," he called to the sheriff. "Let's be heading home."

From the direction of the gorge suddenly sounded fast hoofs. An instant later a man rode into view. His horse was lathered with sweat and flecked with foam.

"Hey, sheriff!" he shouted at sight of Horton, "Cartina held up the San Rosita stage this mawnin'. Killed the driver and creased yore deputy. They got away with the Humboldt's payroll money!"

Chapter XI

AFTER the posse had departed at a gallop, Hatfield dismounted at Bowers' invitation.

"Callate yuh're the feller what went to work for the Boss," he commented, running his keen gaze over the Ranger's tall form. "One of the boys from the ranch rode up here yest'day afternoon and mentioned yuh," he added by way of explanation. "Figgered it couldn't be anybody else when I set eyes on yuh, from the way he d'scribed yuh. C'mon inter my shack. I was jest gettin' ready to have a bit of chuck when that jughaid of a sheriff happened along."

The "shack" was a comfortable one-story house. It had two large rooms and a kitchen. An ancient Mexican was laying a cloth on a table in the main room. While Hatfield was washing up in the kitchen, Bowers talked in low tones with the old Mexican cook in the main room. Hatfield could hear the rumble of voices but could not make out what was said. After placing food on the table, the Mexican drifted silently out the back door and vanished in the direction of the mine. A little later, the Ranger heard hoofs click away toward the lower gorge mouth.

The meal was good and both did ample justice to it. For some minutes there was eloquent silence. Over a final cup of coffee, Bowers became more communicative.

"That blankety-blank sheriff!" he growled. "He means well, I reckon, but he's got one of them single-cinch minds and when he gets what he callates is a idea, there ain't room for nothin' else till it's plumb worked out."

"He's been chasin' Pedro Cartina for more'n a year now and ain't never come within' shootin' distance of him. I callate Cartina is really responsible for 'bout one third of what Horton blames him for. If a rooster gets lifted outa a coop or a greaser goes to sleep and wakes up 'thout his pants, Horton yells 'Cartina!' and c'lects a posse and goes ridin'. When Cartina really does figger on pullin' somethin', like he did this mawnin', he arranges for Horton to be gallivantin' 'round somewhere else on a tip that's all made to order.

"The only time Horton was anyways close to him was t'other evenin' when the bank was robbed, and then he was as far behind as a cow's tail. I don't see what John Chadwick sees in the potbellied galoot. Reckon he figgers 'cause Horton can get them shoulders of his under a hoss and lift it off the ground, he's got the makin's of a peace officer. Anyhow, he got Horton elected and is figgerin' on runnin' him for 'nother term."

"Lift a horse off the ground?" repeated the Ranger.

"Uh-huh, he can do that. Horton's a bull when it comes to bein' strong. There ain't a man in the district can give him a good go in a rassle, 'less it's the Boss, Amado Capistrano. There ain't anythin' much Capistrano can't do with them arms of his. Jest the same, bein' able to straighten hoss shoes, and lift kegs of spikes with yore teeth ain't all what's nec'sary to make a good peace officer. Brains sorta comes in handy at times, and Horton was down in the cellar when they was handin' *them* out. Oh, well, what can yuh 'spect of sich a tailend of Creation as this section is!"

"You don't like this country?"

"Who would like it?" growled Bowers, a bitter light

119

in his stormy eyes. "The only reason I'm here, runnin' a blankety-blank silver mine is 'cause I got to be."

Hatfield was glancing at the titles of the books that rested on shelves built against the walls.

"You're an engineer." he stated rather than asked.

The bitter light in Bowers' eyes grew intense.

"Was," he corrected. "Ever hear of the Talmapaso River bridge?"

Hatfield nodded.

"Well," continued Bowers, "you'll recollect the span went into the river the day after it was completed. Three men were killed. That finished me as an engineer in this country. Was gettin' ready to starve or go back to punchin' cows at forty per when Amado Capistrano give me this job."

Hatfield was much interested.

"I remember there was quicksand under the center pier of the Talmapaso Bridge and it shifted," he commented.

Bowers gave him a shrewd glance in which was something of an element of surprise, and perhaps some other emotion.

"Yes, that's right," he said, and as he spoke his voice underwent a subtle change, the careless slurring of the cow country sluffing off and final endings taking their proper places.

"Yes, that's right," he repeated. "The general consensus of opinion and the verdict of the investigating board was that I did not sink my caissons deep enough, and I was judged accordingly. The truth of the matter was that springs opened up through fissures in the bed rock and changed a perfect foundation of hard packed sand to quicksand. Perhaps you can understand what that means?"

"I get the idea," Hatfield replied in his easy drawl. Bowers shrugged.

"But that's water over the dam," he added, his tones changing again. "Callate I'm lucky to have this job. It pays well and the work's sorta int'restin', partickler since some galoot's figger'd out a scheme to rustle highgrade ore outa the diggin's."

"You installed the conveyor system, didn't you?" Hatfield remarked.

"Uh-huh. Puttin' up a mill here in the hills was mighty near outa the question, and packin' ore down by mules is slow and costly. The conveyors are a sight faster and cheaper. The other mines have 'em, too."

After that they smoked in silence. Bowers appeared to be brooding over the past and his clever, bad-tempered face grew more and more morose. Finally he pinched out his cigarette and rose to his feet.

"Gotta be lookin' things over," he said, "wanta come along?"

Hatfield hesitated a moment.

"I guess I've got time," he admitted at length.

Together they entered the shaft cage and were dropped plummet like into the depths of the mine. Here they walked along endless gloomy galleries. High overhead, for hundreds of feet, stretched the intricate cribbing of heavy timbers that held apart the sides of the gutted lode. It was like to the picked bones of the giant skeleton of some prehistoric monster, with lights that were the lamps of the miners flickering about among the bleached ribs and vertebrae. Most of the workers, Hatfield noted, were Mexicans. As was his custom, he scanned closely each face that came into view under the dim lights. Most were of the humble *peon* type, with scant intelligence showing in the dark eyes.

Rounding an abrupt turn, they came upon a group of pickmen bringing down a face of rock previously shattered by dynamite. A scrawny little fellow glanced up from his work and Hatfield caught a flicker of stark terror in the beady eyes. Without comment he passed on, apparently lending an attentive ear to Bowers' comments but in reality hearing little of what was said.

For in the scrawny little pickman he had recognized the man he had rescued from the grip of the Tamarra Desert, the man who had vanished into the rainy night, hugging to his breast a new government-model rifle. He had also noticed that Joseph Bowers, the mine superintendent, had nodded to the little laborer in a familiar fashion and had received a nod in return.

This, and certain peculiarities he had noted about the mysterious rifle, were occupying the Lone Wolf's mind as the shaft cage rose to the surface. He was still thinking about them when he bade Bowers good day and rode slowly toward the lower gorge. The bitter-eyed superintendent stared after him speculatively.

"And *what* are *you?*" Bowers muttered as the tall form vanished around a bend. "Funny thing, a wandering cowboy who knows about the Talmapaso Bridge disaster and understands how quicksand could form under a pier. The boss and me had better have a little gabfest. And there won't be any slip-up this time!"

At the same instant Jim Hatfield's mind was going back to that hot day not so long ago when he had stared up at the masked face of a tall, broad-shouldered man while the hot jaws of the ants nipped his flesh; a man whose eyes had been bright and burning in the shadow of his wide hat.

He had conclusively recognized Bowers as the tall man who had fled from Flintlock Horner's livery stable as the Ranger's gun hammers clicked on empty shells. He wondered if Bowers suspected that his identity was known.

Hatfield was inclined to doubt it, feeling that his own dissimulation had been too real. But either way, Jim Hatfield knew that truly he rode in the very shadow of Death's wing.

For the Lone Wolf's keen eyes had noted something else—something that vastly complicated the whole matter; something that opened up such possibilities that his breath caught at thought of them. And that "something" was nothing more startling than the film of gray dust on Sheriff Horton's hat!

Chapter XII

HATFIELD rode swiftly down the gorge, for the sun was already slanting low toward the west. He followed the conveyor line most of the way, but veered away from it as the track entered the narrow gut where the canyon opened onto the dry wash.

For nearly half a mile the trail ran under a steep slope that extended for a thousand yards or more upward toward the splintered faces of towering cliffs. This slope, of loose shale and crumbling earth, was strewn with boulders, many of them weighing tons. The far side of the gut was a sheer granite wall, at the base of which was a dry watercourse which would be a raging torrent in time of rain. The gut itself was not much over a hundred yards in width, its floor uneven, broken by ridges and hummocks and littered with boulders and float.

Carefully Goldy picked his way amid the treacherous rocks. It would be easy to turn a hoof here and the sorrel knew it. Hatfield eyed the ominous slope thoughtfully, wary of rocks loosened by vibrations of the blasting at the mine.

"Wouldn't take much to set the whole mess rolling down," he mused. He was almost a quarter of the distance through the gut.

Without warning, smoke mushroomed from the base of the cliff that crowned the slope. There was a yellowish flash and a shattering roar. A huge section of the cliff bulged outward, seemed to hang for an instant and then toppled forward with a deafening crash. Down the slope rushed the splintered mass, gathering an increment of shale and loose boulders. In a few seconds, the entire surface of the slope was in motion.

One swift glance and Hatfield yelled to his horse. The big sorrel shot forward, heedless of the treacherous footing beneath his hoofs. The terrible rumbling roar and the billowing dust clouds up the slope lent frantic speed to the racing mount. Hugging his long body to the ground, he fairly poured himself over the shifting rubble, and with every breathless second, the thundering avalanche rolled closer to the doomed pair.

Ahead, far ahead, was the widening mouth of the gut, and safety, but Hatfield knew the straining horse could never make it. Already boulders and fragments of shale that had outstripped the main body of the avalanche were whizzing past, striking the floor of the gut with terrific force and bounding on to shatter against the cliffs on the far side. He knew that in another few seconds the thundering mass would pour into the gut, destroying all that lay in its path.

Hatfield veered Goldy toward the cliff wall, as far away from the moving slope as possible, but there was no hope of safety there. The main body of the avalanche undoubtedly would roll to the foot of the cliffs, shattering them with a barrage of stones as deadly as an artillery bombardment. There was not one chance in a million for horse or rider to escape the rain of bounding missiles.

All this flashed through the Ranger's mind as the horse sped forward. He glanced up at the billowing dust clouds, through which the boulders whizzed and leaped, at the cliff on his right and then down the gut.

Ahead, a hundred yards or so distant, was a low hillock, a rocky uprearing that swelled from the floor of the gut almost equidistant from the slope and the cliff wall. Its sides were precipitous, its summit a wind smoothed knob of granite.

Hatfield turned the sorrel slightly. Straight at the almost perpendicular side of the hillock he sent the flying horse. Goldy snorted explosively and it seemed that certainly he would crash in red ruin against the craggy base.

But like a mountain goat he took the dizzy rise. Scratching, clinging, the muscles of his powerful haunches swelling in mighty bands, he went up the slope, carried forward by the impetus of his mad gallop. The instant he began to falter, Hatfield left the saddle in a lithe movement of consummate grace. Together, man and horse strained and scrambled up the rise. Not until they reached the base of the rounded knob did they pause. Facing about, his back against the smooth stone that towered many feet above his head, the Ranger watched the roaring rush of the avalanche as it thundered onto the floor of the gut and rolled onward toward the cliff wall.

It reached the hillock, coiled about it, splitting like a wave of water on a rugged reef. Up and up piled the mass of stone and earth, reaching with splintered fingers toward the crouching man and horse. Nearer and nearer, straining to flow over the resisting granite and engulf the hillock. A mighty blast of air flattened them against the knob and threatened to whirl them from their refuge like leaves in an autumn gale. It shrieked and howled about the knob, adding its clamor to the booming voices of the avalanche. Up and up piled the flowing earth and shale.

In the wake of the main body of the avalanche came great boulders loosened from their beds of centuries. Faster and faster they rolled, whirling, bounding, leaping high into the air. They battered the hillock, tearing away tons of stone from its rugged sides, filling the air full of flying splinters that were deadly as rifle bullets. One hurtled through the air and struck squarely on the crest of the knob. It shattered the knob and burst into a thousand fragments which went whizzing away, each singing its own wild song. Stone from the splintered knob rained about Hatfield and the sorrel and some small fragments struck them stinging blows.

That was the last supreme effort of the avalanche. Gradually the clamor died. The dust clouds settled. Occasional boulders still whizzed down, bursting like meteors through the dust fog, but they grew less frequent. The air cleared and Hatfield, watching intently, could see the cliffs above the slope. He had drawn his rifle from the saddle boot and abruptly he flung it to his shoulder. He had sensed movement in the shadow at the base of the cliff.

The rifle muzzle held level with rock-like steadiness. Hatfield's eyes, coldly gray, glanced along the sights. Goldy snorted as the clanging, metallic crash of the report echoed back and forth among the crags.

Again the rifle spoke, and again, the flashes palely golden in the dying sunshine, the smoke whisping up from the muzzle in blue spirals.

High against the cliff face a puff of dust sprang into the air, and another as Hatfield's slugs struck the rock wall. Then there was an answering flash from a gun and a blue spiral of smoke wavered against the white surface of the cliff.

Before the crack of the report reached Hatfield's ears, a bullet spatted viciously against the knob less than a foot above his head. An instant later a second slug fanned his face with its deadly breath.

"The fellow can shoot," he muttered, changing his position slightly, "almost as good as he can blow down rocks. *Now* where is he?"

Outlined against the sun drenched knob, he was at a distinct disadvantage, the unknown rifleman being in the shadow. Suddenly he saw the bright flicker of flame in the pool of shadow and with a quick glance along the sights he fired in reply.

A slug whined past and whanged against the knob, but Jim Hatfield hardly noticed it. His whole attention was centered on the dark figure that was bounding and rolling down the steep slope.

"I guess that will hold him!" grated the Lone Wolf, lowering his smoking rifle.

Down and down bounded the limp body, setting shale and loose boulders rolling as it came. The body was the nucleus of a miniature avalanche when it finally came to rest amid the heaped rubble on the gorge floor.

Picking his way carefully over the wild jumble the avalanche had left in its wake, Hatfield led his horse down the hillock which had provided a haven of refuge and reached the spot where the body lay half buried in rock rubbish. He hauled it forth and stared at what had once been a small man.

So battered and mangled was it by its fall down the slope, that it was impossible to do little more than imagine what the man had looked like in life. The features were a raw smear of bloody flesh and every bone in the man's body seemed to have been shattered. The dark skin of one wrinkled hand pointed to Mexican or Indian blood; the black hair was plentifully shot with gray.

"An oldish fellow, I reckon," the Ranger mused, "and he was a Mexican, all right. Wonder if there's anything in his clothes that'll tell something about him?"

A careful search revealed little. The rifle, of course, was missing and an empty holster was evidence that a six-gun had fallen out on the way down the slope. One cartridge belt was still in place and Hatfield examined the shells with intense interest. They were the type of cartridges designed for just such a rifle as the wizened little Mexican had hugged to his breast that wild night on the Tamarra Desert, but Hatfield was convinced that the broken body before him was not that of the mysterious little man.

"Looks like there's an arsenal of those tong guns loose hereabouts," he mused, dropping the cartridge into his pocket.

He glanced about the gut, noting that the conveyor lines were down in a wild jumble of tangled cables, battered buckets and splintered poles. Hatfield knew that crews would soon be hurrying from the mills and the mines to repair the damage. He did not wish the body of the dead dynamiter to be found at this spot.

To carry the mangled form in his arms would mean blood smears on both himself and his horse, so he flipped the loop of his lariat about the crumpled shoulders and drew the body after him as he rode up the gut and beyond the havoc wrought by the avalanche. He buried the body in a crack between two rocks and weighted it down with boulders. Then he rode up the slope toward the base of the cliffs which overhung the scene of the avalanche. The grade was steep, but here it was grown with brush and grass and Goldy had little trouble keeping his footing.

In a hollow, a few hundred yards from where the cliff had been dynamited, Hatfield found what he sought—the dynamiter's horse. For long minutes he studied the brand which marked the animal and his eyes were cold as the winter wind in the tops of the pines.

"It's beginning to tie up," he muttered at last. "Yes,

it's beginning to tie up. Ed Shafter sowed the seed, and there's going to be a mighty surprising reaping hereabouts before long!"

He relieved the horse of saddle and bridle and left it to shift for itself. After concealing the equipment, he rode through the hills until he could descend into the dry wash. A little later he met the first group of repairmen from the mills. He gave them directions to the seat of the trouble and rode on, not mentioning his own hair-raising experience. The first stars of evening were glowing in the quiet sky as he rode along the main street of Helidoro.

And from the *Una Golondrina* saloon, startled, incredulous eyes watched him swing from the saddle and hitch his horse. Before he entered the saloon, hurrying feet padded away through the dark.

Jim Hatfield was not thinking of furtive footsteps or watching eyes as he entered the One Swallow saloon. He was thinking of *the dust on Sheriff Horton's black hat!*

Chapter XIII

AMADO CAPISTRANO was not present. Hatfield had something to eat, and then went in search of Walsh, the banker. He found him working in his little office in the front of the bank.

"Capistrano has always lived in this section," the banker replied to Hatfield's question. "His family once owned the entire valley. They lost it through court decisions relating to the old Spanish grants. Amado was only a child then. That was during John Chadwick's first term in the legislature. I have heard that Chadwick was instrumental in instigating the judicial action.

"Anyway, there is no love lost between him and the Capistranos. Chadwick bought up all the land he was able to at the time. Since then he has acquired other slices of the valley. I believe his ambition is to acquire the whole of it. Capistrano has some such ambition himself, in my opinion. Chadwick was furious when Capistrano got the jump on him and bought the Widow Bloodsoe's property right from under his nose. John's a good man, but he has the failing of men who have always got what they wanted—he feels that it is actually wrong for anybody to oppose him in anything.

"Nobody ever paid much attention to Amado Capistrano until he made his silver strike in the hills. He's a rich man now, but it doesn't seem to have changed him any. His saloon is the hangout of a lot of questionable characters, but Amado doesn't seem to mix with them much. Horton has more than once intimated that he has a connection with Pedro Cartina. It has never been proven."

"Does Chadwick own mining property?" Hatfield asked.

"He has a controlling interest in the Lucky Turn and the Humboldt," Walsh replied "They're good mines, but not so rich as the Cibola. That's the ace of the district. The Humboldt has been doing well of late, I understand."

In answer to another question, Walsh stated:

"Yes, there's a telegraph station at San Rosita. It's about eighteen miles southeast of here, right on the river. Take the San Simon Trail, the one the stage follows. By the way, the stage was held up this morning by Cartina, they say. Long John Dyson says he recognized Cartina, said he had his shoulder bandaged and shot with his left hand. They knocked Long John off the box before he could use his shotgun, split his scalp but didn't do him much damage. Killed the driver and escaped with the Humboldt payroll money.

"I'm thankful it wasn't in the bank's hands yet. The express company is responsible. That's twice the Humboldt has lost money. They got the Lucky Turn payroll about six weeks ago. Cartina shows uncanny skill in picking times when the stage is carrying money—and that information is not given out for general consumption."

"I imagine not," Hatfield agreed. "Express company lose in those other holdups, too?"

"Yes. The company is responsible for the money while it is in transport. It has suffered heavy loss, due to these robberies. I have expected they would assign one of their operatives to this district, but—"

He broke off suddenly, regarding the tall Ranger with newly aroused interest. Hatfield read the question in the little man's honest eyes. He smiled down at Walsh from his great height and slowly shook his head.

"No, I'm not working for the express company," he said softly.

He eyed the banker speculatively for a moment and arrived at a swift decision. He needed someone upon whom he could rely, who could be depended upon to supply needed information freely and accurately. His slim hand fumbled inside his shirt for a moment and laid a shining object on the banker's desk.

Walsh stared at the familiar silver star on a silver circle, that badge of courage and efficiency. He drew a long breath.

"A Ranger!" he exclaimed, almost to himself. "I might have known it the first time I clapped eyes on you. Now we'll get somewhere!"

He immediately gave Hatfield a letter to the bank in Santa Rosita.

"Now you will be able to use their private wire to send your telegrams," he explained. "Information is much less liable to leak out that way. Men of Cartina's ilk appear to have an uncanny ability to ferret out what's going on. I can't understand how they do it. This ought to help you keep things secret. Hardy, president of the Santa Rosita bank, is absolutely dependable—I'll stake my life on that. He'll do all he can to help you."

Hatfield was still unable to locate Amado Capistrano. The barkeepers at the saloon knew nothing of his whereabouts. Long John Dyson, Sheriff Horton's gangling deputy, who happened in a little later with a bandaged head, could supply no information as to the

134

hunchback's whereabouts. Hatfield liked Long John, who had a weary face, a cast in one eye and a discouraged looking moustache. An habitual twinkle made one forget the cast, however, and the moustache could not hide the grin wrinkles about his mouth.

Not until Doc Draper bustled in for a double slug of his "fav'rite pizen," did Hatfield get a line on Capistrano.

"Shore, I know where he is," grunted Ol' Doc. "Come along and I'll take yuh to him."

He led the way to where the humble cabins of the Mexican laborers crouched in the shadow of the great mills. He entered a dimly lighted hut. Hatfield, bending his tall head, followed.

At first he could make out little of the interior. Then he saw that a man and a woman stood near the table on which a lamp burned. They were young and the woman's face was beautiful, though tear-stained and tired. Doc nodded briefly and they replied with courteous bows. Hatfield followed the old man's gaze and saw, in one corner, a blanket spread on the earthen floor. On the blanket lay a wasted little form and beside the blanket crouched Amado Capistrano, his face lined with weariness, but with a light in his blue eyes. He smiled fleetingly at Hatfield and raised his right hand to his lips in a gesture for silence.

His other hand, Hatfield saw, lay on the worn blanket and in it rested the tiny, almost transparent fingers of the little girl who slept so silently on the earthen floor. The fragile fingers clung tightly to the hunchback's thumb, as if that were their sole hold on the life spirit that threatened momentarily to take wing.

"He's been settin' there for nigh onto eighteen hours now," breathed Doc. "If he moves he's 'fraid the kid'll wake up, and sleep means life to her. She's been hangin' in the balance for a week, now, but yest'day she drifted into a nacherel sleep while Amado was holdin' her hand. That sleep's gonna make her all right, or I'm much mistaken."

He nodded to Capistrano and led the Ranger from the cabin. A little distance from the door they paused and glanced back.

"Folks down here think sorta well of *Don* Amado," Doc remarked.

Jim Hatfield bared his dark head and looked up at the glowing Texas stars.

"And I guess the folks up *there* think right well of him, too," he replied softly.

"Who?" asked Doc, in surprise.

"Those grand old ancestors of his," Hatfield said. "Those salty old hombres they called the Conquistadores, who came from across the Atlantic and fought the Indians and the deserts and the mountains and did their part to make this country worth living in. Yes, I have a notion *they* think mighty well of *Don* Amado, too. Doc, I reckon that when God Almighty sets out to make a *man,* he concentrates on what He puts inside and doesn't waste too much time on what He covers it up with!"

Chapter XIV

HATFIELD slept at the A Bar C bunkhouse that night and mid morning found him riding the range again. As previously, he headed southwest, but once he was well away from the home range, he turned Goldy's head sharply. An hour later he struck the San Simon Trail, that ran southeast to the county seat, Santa Rosita.

Arriving at Santa Rosita, he found the bank president, Hardy, and showed him Burton Walsh's letter. Hardy cooperated gladly and Hatfield sent several long telegrams in the name of the Rangers. One, directed to an eastern firearms manufacturer, was answered promptly, Hatfield receiving the information he desired before nightfall. It caused him to knit his dark brows and stare long and earnestly across the gleaming river that separated Texas from Mexico. The others were briefly acknowledged and cooperation promised.

Following Hardy's directions, he strolled about the little town, finally arriving at the poorer quarter, occupied chiefly by Mexicans and a few Indians. Here he had a drink in a dingy little *cantina* whose dark-faced bartender grinned jovially and was inclined to be loquacious.

"I've been looking for a bunky of mine," Hatfield told him over a glass of fiery *tequila*. "He headed down this way about a year or so back and I heard he was seen in this town. He was a mining man, a big fellow with brown whiskers sort of dappled. There was gray in his hair, too. Wasn't very old, though. Name was Shafter, Ed Shafter."

The bartender listened courteously, nodding his sleek black head from time to time.

"Me, I know not for sure," he replied when Hatfield had finished. "Many men come thees way and many men drink here. I will ask of others, however, and if the señor should pass this way tomorrow—"

"Yes, I reckon I'll be hanging around this section another day or two," Hatfield told him. "Let's have another drink. Then I'm goin' to bed."

The bartender had learned nothing the following afternoon and Hatfield left town, assuring the drink mixer that he would return in a few days. The young Mexican pocketed the shining gold piece the Ranger had left and redoubled his inquiries.

Hatfield reached the A Bar C bunkhouse after dark. An animated discussion was under way, the subject being a raid on the Bowtie ranch by rustlers. It appeared a herd of several hundred head had been widelooped.

"They figger it was Pedro Cartina did it?" asked the Ranger.

There was a sudden silence and an uncomfortable shuffling of feet. Hatfield glanced inquiringly from one *vaquero* to another. The jolly Felipe at length broke the silence.

"Eet ees, what you call, sometimes not healthy to

speak of certain ones," he said gravely. Hatfield nodded his understanding.

"Yes, you never know who you can trust and who you can't," he agreed.

The next day Hatfield rode across Chadwick's great Circle C and far east. Everywhere he was struck by the richness of the valley. The ranches were exceptionally fine, with splendid buildings, and fat herds in abundance.

"Yes, it sure is one fine section," he mused as he rode slowly home under the glowing stars. "No wonder Chadwick and Capistrano both have a hankering to own the whole business. Plenty of room for both of them, too, and no real need for trouble. Seems that when a man has about everything in the world he needs, he should be satisfied and not be taking chances with what he's got to get something more that he doesn't really need. Funny folks in this world!"

In the beginning, just prior to the death of a young Ranger by the name of Dick Webb, three men had dreamed of an empire. That is, at least one of them had dreamed of an empire, while the other two had envisioned wealth and power in the Tamarra Hills country.

This dream, this will o' the wisp which has beckoned men down through the ages to their doom, was now by way of becoming a concrete fact. At the same moment that Ranger Jim Hatfield, the pernicious fly in this particular ointment, was riding east of the Circle C and deliberating on the intricate pieces of this puzzle which were gradually falling into place for him, two of these three men were closeted with a third man in the back room of a saloon in the mining town of Helidoro. The third member of this infamous trio was absent.

The saloon in which this meeting occurred was not the *Una Golondrina* of Amado Capistrano. Further, not one of the three men in conference was masked. One of them walked the streets of Helidoro whenever he was in town, a respected citizen and officer of the law. Sheriff Branch Horton was cradled in false security, little dreaming that Jim Hatfield had already penetrated that mask of respectability.

The second member was, oddly enough, the very man that Sheriff Horton could never lay an official hand upon—Pedro Cartina. He had ridden into town under cover of darkness the previous night for a conference. He sat in his chair now, a vicious scowl on his swarthy face, wincing now and then from pain as he shifted his bandaged right shoulder.

The third man in the room, the one making a worried report, was Jefferson Bowers, superintendent of the Cibola mine.

"I can't understand how he come outa it in one piece," Bowers stated in perplexity. "I examined that cut myself, and it's piled fulla rock and dirt enough to wipe out a regiment. When yuh sent me word, Horton, that he had showed up in town as if nothin' had happened, I couldn't believe it."

"I couldn't believe it," snarled the sheriff, and there was nothing slow about his bearing now. "Yuh said yuh could tend to him, before I left for town with my posse, so I didn't worry any more about him till he showed up life-size. Mebbe yore dynamite man can explain things. What did he say?"

"That's the queerest part of it," frowned Bowers. "Just before supper I gave Juan definite instructions and sent him on ahead of Amado's new man. There ain't no doubt that Juan did the job—nothin' short of dynamite would of caused that avalanche, and Juan was the best powder man I had at the mine. But Juan has disappeared. Nobody's seen hair or hide of him since that job."

"Perhaps Juan failed," shrugged Cartina, and then cursed at the quick little pain which gnawed at his shoulder. "When he saw he had failed, he vamosed to Mexico."

"Juan knew better than to do that," said Bowers. "He knew yuh'd get him for that, Cartina. It begins to look to me like, somehow, that big fellow got Juan."

Pedro Cartina smiled, a swarthy grin that split his face wolfishly to expose gleaming white teeth.

"Then, señores," he said, "it seems that the job must be done by Cartina himself. Do you still think he is a detective from the express company?"

"Must be," grunted Horton. "He don't fit in as a driftin' range tramp like he claimed to be. I wish yuh'd shot him out of his saddle, Pedro, when yuh raided Walsh's bank that night."

"It was dark," said Cartina, "and we just took him for a rider who was in our way."

"He proved to be that, all right," said Horton sourly. "The boss was sore over that bobble."

"He's not an express detective," said Bowers positively. "I think he's a Cattlemen's Association man. Sancho swears he's the feller who pulled him out of the desert the night of the storm, but he said that feller could talk Spanish like a Mex, and this man don't seem to know the lingo. He looked familiar to me, and—"

"He asked Sancho questions about his gun?" demanded Horton quickly.

"Shore," nodded Bowers. "And I'm beginnin' to think that gun-runnin' idea you fellers had was a mistake. They're mighty fine shootin' irons all right, but they might be traced. If they are, we'll have the U. S. army in this section."

"Not so," said Cartina smoothly. "The guns were shipped to my friend, the captain of the *Rurales,* and the ordair was from the Department of War, or State, or so it seemed. There is nothing to fear from that source."

"Well, there's a lot to fear from this man we can't kill," said Bowers in an ugly tone. "Cartina, I tell yuh I recognized—"

"Everythin' else is workin' out fine," cut in the sheriff, relieved. "The boys are learnin' to shoot straighter. They know their business. There's more'n a hundred of 'em now. They have their orders, and they know what to do. Another week, and we'll be ready for big clean-ups. As soon as this election is out of the way, we'll get goin' right. There might be a few men we ain't shore of—"

He paused and glanced at Cartina, who smiled again—like the unsheathing of a knife.

"I am sure of all," the Mexican said thinly. "Men think twice before they hand to Pedro Cartina the, what you say—doublecross."

"Yeah," nodded Sheriff Horton in satisfaction, "I guess they do."

"Now, for this detective," went on Cartina, "I, Pedro Cartina, will attend to him without more ado. Me, I am able to dispose of men so they do not come back to life."

"Yeah?" said Bowers dryly. "Mebbe yuh are. But I'm tryin' to tell yuh that yuh already had one whack at this man, and yuh made a mess of it."

"What?" hissed Cartina, his black eyes flashing. "That, amigo, is one damn lie!"

Bowers laughed shortly.

"I told yuh I recognized this Hatfield feller, didn't I? That's why I'm shore he's a cattle detective. Do yuh remember that little raid on the Slash K trail herd down on the Rio Grande which didn't work out because of that tall feller leadin' them cow hands?"

"You mean the hombre we staked out over the ant hill?" demanded Cartina.

"Him," nodded Bowers laconically. "This man is him!"

"But—but—" stuttered the bandit in astonishment, "that is not possible. The ants never fail."

"They fell down on that job!" said Bowers grimly. "I

143

don't know how he got loose. Yuh drove them stakes, and I pigged him with the rawhide myself. If he ever finds out it was me with yuh that day, I won't live till sundown. We ain't safe a minute while that man runs free. Think he'll forget that ant hill?"

"That, as I recall it, was your idea, Señor Bowers," said Cartina in silky politeness. "I preferred to end his career with a rifle then. Now, I must do so. What did you say his name is?"

"Hatfield!" snapped Bowers angrily. "Jim Hatfield, so he says."

Pedro Cartina forgot his wounded shoulder as he leaped to his feet, his face livid, his eyes almost starting from his head.

"Hatfield?" he ejaculated. "Jeem Hatfield! He ees tall, most tall? And broad? And his eyes, they are gray? *Madre de dios! Sangre de cristo! Maldito!*"

"Yes, yes," nodded Bowers, paling slightly in unreasoning panic. "Why?"

"Mother of God!" groaned Cartina. "And to think that I had him under the sights of my rifle and let him get away."

"What are yuh talkin' about?" demanded Sheriff Horton savagely.

"Hatfield!" gasped the bandit. "Of all the men in the world I, Pedro Cartina, most hate and fear, it is this man. You wish to know who he is? You think he is express detective, or cattle detective? Ha, ha, I laugh! Señores, this man is called the Lone Wolf. He is a devil. He is a Texas Ranger!"

"Holy smoke!" exclaimed Bowers, utterly startled.

"Hell!" snarled Sheriff Horton. "Ain't we already killed one Ranger last year—that Webb feller? John Chadwick thinks he can run this country without Texas Rangers nosin' around here. He depends on me, don't he? Ain't he already exerted influence to keep Rangers officially out of Tamarra country? This Hatfield ain't got no official standin' here. We'll treat him like we do everybody who gets in our way."

"Do yuh think Amado knows he hired a Ranger?" asked Bowers keenly.

"'Course not!" snorted Horton. "Think he's crazy? His feud is personal with Chadwick."

"I guess I'd better tell him," said Bowers. "Yuh're shore of yore information, Cartina?"

"Am I?" shuddered the bandit. "Hatfield is the one man I have dreaded having set on my trail."

Sheriff Horton pulled his six-shooter and laid it on the table. His eyes were full of meaning as he looked at both of his companions.

"It wasn't Lincoln who made men equal," he chuckled evilly. "It was Sam Colt! Here's the difference between this Ranger Hatfield and the smallest man who ever forked a hoss."

Pedro Cartina shook his head dubiously.

"Perhaps," he hissed. "But my thought of *el infierno* is this Jeem Hatfield with a pair of guns!"

"He's human, ain't he?" Horton snapped viciously. "This Hatfield feller can die, like anybody else. And he's got to die—sudden!"

Chapter XV

"I WARNED you," Amado Capistrano told Hatfield. "Not for a moment is your life safe. Twice they have failed, partly by luck, chiefly because of your own vigilance and skill. But it can't go on this way. The next time they're liable not to fail. I still think you should leave this district."

"I think things are going to get interesting around here during the next few days," the Ranger countered.

Capistrano nodded gravely.

"Yes, the election campaign is drawing to a close," he said. "Monday night both Horton and I will make speeches here in Helidoro. Then next day is election day.

"Those speeches are important," he added, "Helidoro will just about swing the election. Chadwick is doing everything he can to defeat me, but there is a large element throughout the valley who will vote for anybody who is against Horton, and I believe most of the mining element is favorable to me. Also I count heavily on the river towns. Most of the voters there are of Mexican extraction, although Texas citizens, and naturally favor one of their blood."

"Why does Chadwick set such store on this county election?" Hatfield asked. "It doesn't look so important to me."

"It's a test of strength," Capistrano replied. "This is, and always has been, an independent county. If Chadwick can show the surrounding counties that he can swing Tamarra, it will add tremendously to his prestige. Enough, I feel sure, to gain him the nomination for governor next year."

Hatfield nodded. He was very thoughtful as he sought his little room over the livery stable.

"And if Chadwick gets to be governor, he'll run the state like he runs this valley," the Lone Wolf mused, "and that means goodby to the Rangers, among other things. Goodby to the Rangers, and Chadwick's riders will be all over the state. Such things just don't seem possible; but it doesn't seem possible that a little sore can grow into a cancer that'll kill a man. Just the same, it happens.

"The way to cure a sore is to treat it before it gets too big to *be* cured, even if it doesn't seem worth noticing at first. Wait till it gets big enough to notice, and it's liable to be too big to handle. I'm afraid Chadwick is a sore. Well, the Rangers have cured 'sores' before now. I reckon we can handle this one."

Things were gay in the river town of Zapata. The *cantinas* were decorated with flowers and colored cloth. Svelte señoritas, their dark eyes flashing like jewels, multicolored skirts billowing out from slim silken legs, danced with lithe young *vaqueros* in velvet and silver.

Gay *serapes,* elaborate sombreros and fluttering *mantillas* lent color to the scene. Everywhere was music, and laughter. In the sun-drenched plaza a crowd had gathered to hear the words of the *alcalde.*

The mayor, his dark face wreathed with smiles, spoke from a raised platform—warmly lauding his friend, *Don* Amado Capistrano, who soon would be sheriff of the county.

"It is the great honor to help elect our friend and patron," the *alcalde* said. "Zapata will do her part, as will her sister towns. I ordain this a day of *fiesta*. Tomorrow—"

He paused at a sudden drumming of hoofs growing steadily louder. Persons glanced inquiringly one to another.

"El bandidos?" ran a nervous whisper.

Into the plaza thundered a veritable army of mounted men. There were fully four-score riders. Each carried a heavy rifle of a pattern unusual along the Border. They crashed to a halt and their leader, a rangy, rawboned man with a low-drawn hat brim, rode through the crowd that made way for him. At his back rode two dark-faced, sinewy men. The grim trio halted beside the platform. The tall leader leaned forward in his saddle and addressed the apprehensive mayor.

"Mister," he said harshly, "yuh been barkin' on the wrong side of the fence. Yuh need a lesson."

He gestured to his two dark followers, who instantly swung to the platform and seized the mayor.

An angry mutter ran through the crowd, rising to a sullen growl. Instantly there was a thunderous crash of rifles. Lead squalled over the heads of the crowd. Acrid smoke swirled about the plaza.

Demoralized, panic stricken, the people huddled

together. In the *cantinas* the music was stilled. Shutters closed hastily.

The two men who had seized the mayor ripped the gay silk shirt from his back, baring his shoulders. The tall leader dismounted and vaulted upon the platform, running muscular fingers along the lash of his heavy quirt.

Then the quirt rose, and fell. A red welt leaped across the mayor's dark shoulders. Again the lash whistled through the air, and again. The mayor writhed. An agonized groan burst from his lips. Then a shriek as blood spurted under the lash. The shrieks merged in a gabbling crescendo of screams as the quirt rose and fell.

Finally the rawboned man turned from his moaning victim, flicked drops of blood from his lash and faced the crowd.

"Jest in case yuh folks don't know it," he said harshly, "I'm here to tell yuh we got the right kind of a sheriff in this county right now, and we aim to keep him. Bear that in mind t'morrer."

He swung into the saddle, running his fingers along the blood-soaked quirt.

"All right," he told his followers, glancing at the sun, "get goin'. We got three more towns to visit, then we ride north. Got to be in Helidoro before dark."

In a cloud of dust the grim band thundered away. The stricken people of Zapata crept into their homes, casting many a fearful glance in the direction of that diminishing dust cloud. Shaking men succored the quivering mayor. The *fiesta* had become a tragedy.

Helidoro was also gay as the sun sank in scarlet and gold and the western peaks were ringed about with saffron flame. Crowds jostled in the streets. Other crowds thronged the bars. Roulette wheels whirred busily. Cards slithered and dice galloped across the green cloth. Boots thumped and high heels clicked.

Lithe cowboys from the valley ranches rubbed shoulders with brawny miners. Gamblers in somber black raked hard-earned gold across their tables. Bartenders were too busy to make change; the drinkers too busy to ask for it. Fiddles squeaked and guitars thrummed.

In the streets hastily organized bands blared forth weird discords that were enthusiastically received as music. Everywhere there was a holiday air, for the mines and the ranches had paid off that evening in anticipation of election day on the morrow.

At either end of town was a final political rally. At one end Sheriff Horton, candidate for re-election, held forth. At the opposite end, Amado Capistrano, who was seeking the office of sheriff, planned to address a huge crowd made up chiefly of mill and mine workers. Dark faces were predominant in that crowd and there were more *"vivas"* heard than "hurrahs"!

Jim Hatfield, lounging on the outskirts of the crowd, chuckled to himself.

"Amado's got four times the turnout Horton has," he grinned. "If this is the way things are going in the river towns, he'll win hands down. Looks like Señor

Chadwick might find a tangle in his rope before he's finished."

Excited cheering broke forth, and a moment later Amado Capistrano mounted the low platform and stood smiling his melancholy smile. He began speaking in his musical voice and the crowd hushed expectantly. The western peaks were wreathed in shadow now and the dusk was purply thick.

Hatfield was suddenly conscious of a low drumming filtering out of the deepening dusk. He turned in surprise, his eyes narrowing.

"Horses," he muttered, "lots of them, and coming fast."

Others had heard the sound and were glancing in the direction of the San Simon Trail. The sound swiftly grew louder. Something huge and menacing loomed against the gray surface of the trail.

What happened next did so with paralyzing suddenness. Out of the night burst a compact band of mounted men. Straight for the crowd about the platform they rode, quirting their horses, shouting loudly.

Panic was immediate and universal. Men fought madly to escape the churning hoofs of the horses and the slashing quirts of the riders.

Many fell and were trampled by their frenzied companions or ridden down by the horses. The platform went to pieces with a crash and in the glare of the falling flares, Hatfield saw a rope snake through the air, the loop settling about Amado Capistrano's shoulders. The hunchback was hurled to the ground and jerked along it as the rope tightened.

Jim Hatfield streaked across the intervening space like a flickering shadow. He seized the rope with both sinewy hands and surged backward with all his iron strength. The horse which drew it, just getting under way, faltered in his' stride.

Again the Ranger put forth every ounce of his strength. The muscles of his splendid back and shoulders stood out like writhing snakes. The veins of his forehead were big as cords. One final mighty effort. The saddle girth burst and rider and saddle hurtled to the ground.

The man lit on his head, flopped over on his side and lay with twitching limbs, his neck twisted to a horrid, unnatural angle. Capistrano and the Ranger sprawled together, the coils of the loosened rope tangled about them.

Rifles crashed a volley and lead stormed over the prostrate pair. Yells of agony arose from the milling crowd. Again the rifles crashed, and again cries of pain followed the blast of lead. Hatfield, rolling over on his side, jerked both his guns and emptied them after the fleeing horsemen. Other shots sounded, but the mysterious band was already out of range. The rope wielder, a sinewy young Mexican, appeared to have been their only casualty.

Men from the other end of town were running down the street. As Hatfield helped the badly shaken Capistrano to his feet, Sheriff Horton pounded up.

"It's too bad that you fellers can't hold a political meetin' without turnin' it into a riot!" he bellowed. "What is goin' on here, anyhow?"

Jim Hatfield glanced down at him from his great height.

"Horton," he drawled, "some day you're going to head in the wrong direction so fast you'll meet yourself coming back!"

That night it rained, and all the next day. Toward evening, Amado Capistrano's election headquarters were as gloomy as the day. The river towns had registered a mere trickle of votes, and the turnout of miners in Helidoro was negligible.

"Horton wins, hands down," the hunchback conceded with a wry smile. "I imagine they're having quite a celebration over at the town hall."

Jim Hatfield dropped into the hall a little later. Sheriff Horton, his mouth stretched in a grin of triumph, was speaking from the stage.

"That's all I got to say, boys," he concluded, "I jest say, 'much obliged,' and yuh done yoreselves proud. Now I want yuh to listen to somebody else for a spell. I want yuh to listen to the Honorable John Chadwick, *our next governor!*"

As Chadwick arose from his chair and cheers rocked the building, the Lone Wolf smiled thinly with his lips—his eyes were icy cold—and left the room.

Chapter XVI

TWO DAYS later, Hatfield rode back to Santa Rosita. He found his friend the bartender in the little *cantina* all smiles. Instead of serving Hatfield's drink at the bar, he hurried him to a table in a corner.

"Be pleased to sit, señor," he bobbed. "I will return with the much speed."

Summoning an assistant to take over the bar, he hurried from the room. Hatfield sipped his drink reflectively and waited. Soon the bartender returned. He brought with him a sinewy, dark little man with lank black hair, high cheek bones and glittering black eyes.

"Thees ees Pancho," he introduced. "He would speak with the *señor.*"

Pancho, whom Hatfield placed as an almost pure Yaqui Indian, sat down diffidently and accepted a drink. He stared steadily at the tall Ranger, his black eyes inscrutable. After his first greeting, Hatfield said nothing. He was content to let Pancho begin the conversation. He did so in a surprising manner.

"*Señor,*" he said softly, "the Señor Shafter whom you seek was of the Rangers?"

Hatfield returned the Yaqui's steady gaze.

"What makes you think so?" he parried. Pancho's eyes did not waver.

"The *Señor* Webb, he too was of the Rangers; and," the Yaqui added, "the *Señor* Webb was my friend. He saved my little daughter from the river. *Si,* he was my *amigo.*"

"I begin to understand," replied Hatfield.

Pancho leaned close.

"You, too, tall *señor,* are of the Rangers," he whispered. "Pancho has eyes that see much. Pancho knows! You come to avenge your brothers. *Si,* it is so?"

Hatfield made a quick decision. He decided the little man was trustworthy and his affection for the slain Ranger, Dick Webb, was undoubtedly real. The hatred that burned in his black eyes when he spoke of avenging Webb's murder was too vibrantly real to be simulated.

"Yes, I come to avenge," he replied simply, employing the terms Pancho would understand and appreciate. "I have to find the men that did it."

"Pancho knows," said the Yaqui. "Pancho told the *Señor* Shafter. He departed and returned not. Perhaps the tall *señor* knows where he may be found?"

"Yes, I know where he can be found," Hatfield replied briefly. "It's the men who killed him and Webb I'm interested in, Pancho."

The little Yaqui leaned forward, his eyes glowing.

"Listen, *Señor,*" he whispered. "Listen closely—"

Under cover of darkness, Hatfield and the Yaqui left town. Hatfield rode his tall sorrel horse, but the little tracker trotted easily at his stirrup, scorning the mount Hatfield offered to obtain for him.

"When the *caballo* falls with rolling eyes and

heaving sides, Pancho runs on and is not tired," he declared proudly in Spanish.

"I believe you," Hatfield nodded, glancing at the coiling ropes of muscle that showed plainly through the thin pantaloons the Yaqui wore.

North by west they travelled, under the golden stars that studded the purple-blue vault of the sky; until the stars faded in the dawn of a new day. They were among the gaunt Tamarra Hills now, and as the east brightened Pancho stealthily led the way to the lip of a great hollow brimful with purple shadows.

At Pancho's advice, Hatfield tethered Goldy in a dense thicket. Then he crouched on the lip of the hollow beside the Yaqui and waited while daylight brightened, revealing the hollow to be grass grown and dense with undergrowth. Through the undergrowth ran a trail, twisting up the far slope and vanishing into a dark opening beneath a huge overhang of reddish stone.

"It is there they meet and plan," whispered the Yaqui. "There their stores are kept. It is from there that they ride forth to do evil."

"Regular hole-in-the-wall outfit," muttered Hatfield. "They—say, there's something coming out of there now!"

Tense, eager, the Ranger and the Yaqui tracker watched the long line of loaded pack mules wind from the dark cavern opening. Each mule was half hidden beneath a great rawhide aparejo, or kyack, as cowboys often called the unwieldy pack sacks.

More than a score of the sturdy animals emerged from the cave, trotted across the hollow and vanished over its lip. Beside and behind the mules rode dark-faced, watchful men. When the last had dipped over the lip of the hollow, Pancho turned a bewildered face to the Ranger.

"Señor, I know not what *that* may mean," he said.

"I have a notion, Pancho, and a good hunch," Hatfield replied, his eyes glowing with excitement. "We've got to see inside that cave. I wonder if anybody is left behind on guard."

"No, *señor,* I would say," replied the Yaqui, "but Pancho will soon learn. Wait here!"

Like a stealthy snake he was gone, worming through the undergrowth, vanishing from sight almost instantly. It was half an hour or more before he reappeared.

"*Señor,* there is no one," he reported. "I am sure."

Taking advantage of all possible cover, Hatfield followed him to the cave mouth. It was dark and silent. Pancho pointed out a heap of torches stacked in a cleft beside the entrance. They lighted one and stole along the comparatively narrow tunnel. The tunnel abruptly opened into a wide room with a lofty ceiling. The floor was level and smooth from the action of water in years gone by. Hatfield glanced about with increasing interest. Pancho exclaimed sharply as they approached a wall.

Row on row stood scores of shiny new rifles of the same model as provided for United States Army use but lacking the army stamp and serial numbers.

"They're made in this country, shipped into Mexico to a captain of *rurales,* the manufacturers thinking they're for Mexican Government service," Hatfield explained. "Then they're smuggled back across the line and used to equip this outlaw gang. That way, they don't attract any attention, as they would if they were shipped to somebody this side the Line. I guess each member of the gang is responsible for the gun issued to him and catches plenty if anything happens to it. That's why that little Mex I found with one in the desert was so scared about it getting away from him."

Pancho nodded his understanding. He pointed to a stack of heavy square boxes.

"Cartridges," Hatfield replied. "That's the kind of box I saw on the mules the night I was shot at there on the Huachuca Trail. I stumbled on part of this outfit and they let drive at me."

They were working their way toward the back of the great room. A moment later Hatfield gave an exclamation of satisfaction. He indicated two heavy cables stretching from a narrow gallery that opened onto the main room.

"That's just what I suspected," he exulted. "Pancho, those mules we saw were loaded with ore from the Cibola mine. It comes in over those cables, somehow. Let's go see how it's done."

They lighted another torch and entered the gallery. For nearly a mile they followed it, the cables stretching on overhead. Pancho suddenly uttered a sharp grunt. Both halted instinctively.

Almost at their feet yawned a dark gulf that seemed to be bottomless. Hatfield kicked a stone over the edge and, long moments later, a faint, muffled splash hissed up to them from the black depths.

"Lord, what a hole!" growled the Ranger, "and look at the trail that leads past it."

Hugging the sheer wall was a narrow track over which the cables passed on supporting piles sunk into the crumbling stone.

Gingerly, they edged out onto the ledge. For nearly a hundred yards it skirted the gulf. Then the unbroken floor of the gallery began once more. A slight distance further on the natural tunnel widened and the torch light revealed the simple but ingenious method utilized for robbing the Cibola mine of high-grade ore.

Twin lines of cables similar to the conveyor lines stretching down the canyon and the wash to Helidoro ran toward the graying opening which was the cleft Hatfield had noted when examining the spilled ore beneath the conveyor line. There was a simple switch and cutback which could easily splice into the main conveyor lines. Along this cutback, loaded buckets of ore could be detoured from the conveyor line and other buckets loaded with base rock switched onto the line in their place. The buckets of rich ore were routed along the cables to the great room where the guns and ammunition were kept. There they were rifled of their precious contents and worthless rock substituted. The

scheme was disarmingly simple, once it was understood.

"But it took a mighty smart engineer to figure that
out," declared Hatfield. "I suppose this tunnel through
the hills was taken into consideration when the conveyor lines were run. I wondered, the first time I saw
them, why they swung over here by the cliffs. It would
have been a more direct route to have run them further
south."

The torch was burning low and they hurried back
toward the main cave. Hatfield took time, however, to
closely examine the crumbling ledge which skirted the
gulf. The huge overhang of stone at the cavern mouth
also excited his interest. He stared at it with calculating eyes and studied the trail that dipped across the
hollow.

"When they're all here, it means nearly a hundred
fighting men, well armed and ready for anything," he
mused. "Routing them out and putting them under
arrest would be a mighty bloody business and peace
officer's blood isn't to be wasted. Maybe a little brains
will take the place of it."

Again he studied the overhang and at the same time
visualized the crumbling ledge. He chuckled as the
plan unfolded; then explained it to Pancho.

The little Yaqui's eyes snapped.

"It will be simple, *señor*," he declared. "You, *señor*,
and I will do the work in the dark hours, both here and
within the cave. Fear not of chance discovery, *Capitan*. None may approach without Pancho knowing."

Which doubtless explained the trip Jim Hatfield and the Yaqui made to the gloomy hollow the following night. They carried mysterious packages with them, which they handled gingerly, and during the space between a sun and a sun they worked at the cavern mouth and on the crumbling ledge.

"It's all ready," the Ranger said at length, straightening his weary back and setting aside drill and sledge. "You'll handle this end when the time comes and I'll take care of the ledge. You're sure you can find out when they'll ride this way again?"

"Pancho will know," the Yaqui replied tersely. "Even now he hurries beyond the river, there to listen and watch. He will warn *El Capitan* in time."

"And after that things will be a lot better in this district," the Ranger commented.

"*Si, Capitan,* and my friend, the young Señor Webb, will sleep more soundly, doubtless."

Jim Hatfield nodded, his eyes grayly cold. He was thinking of a lonely grave beneath the whispering pines close by the bloody Huachuca Trail.

Chapter XVII

THREE nights later Jim Hatfield sat in the *Una Golondrina* and talked with Amado Capistrano. The hunchback was recounting his discovery of the silver lode which became the Cibola mine.

"It was the merest chance," he said. "Had the rabbit darted the other way, I would have cut straight across the canyon toward the Huachuca Trail and never have approached the ledge. I owe much to that rabbit, and I feel, somehow, that I also owe much to a strange and likeable character I met with that same day.

"He was a tall man, nearly as tall as yourself, with a great brown beard shot with gray and fine eyes. He gave me coffee and appeared not to notice my misshapen body. I have often wondered what became of him.

"Strange, on the ledge which was the outcropping of the Cibola lode, I found the marks of a pick, very fresh marks, and I have often wondered did not that kindly stranger stumble upon the rich find before I? If so, why did he not return to claim what was rightly his? There were no notices posted, and no location filed. I searched the records and could find none. Nor could I learn anything of whom the man might be."

"You'll never see him again, *Don* Amado," Hatfield replied softly, "and I guess you were right in thinking he hit on your ledge, too. I happen to know," he added, "that fellow, whose name was Shafter, left an old mother without much to live on."

Amado Capistrano glanced up at the tall Ranger, a warm light in his clear eyes. He smiled his charming, melancholy smile.

"You make me very happy, my friend," he said. "That old mother will never know want, nor lack with the material things to make happy the declining years. Now tell me—"

The talk was suddenly interrupted by a man who

came striding across the dance floor. It was John Chadwick, wearing a jovial smile. He stopped at the table occupied by Hatfield and the hunchback.

"Amado," he said, "I've been doing some thinking. There isn't one bit of sense in you and I being on the prod against each other the way we have been. Supposing we call it quits and try and get along together?"

Capistrano smiled his reply.

"Nothing would appeal to me more," he declared heartily.

"Fine!" exclaimed Chadwick. "Tell you what—supposing you come over to my place tomorrow, about noon. It isn't but about three hours' ride, you know. We'll have a little talk and thrash things out proper. You come along, too, Hatfield. I've got a bottle or two of the right stuff and my Mex cook puts up a mighty fine meal. What do you say? Is it a go?"

He rested his broad hands on the table top and leaned forward as he spoke. His coat swung open and Hatfield could see the guns in his carefully adjusted shoulder holsters. His gaze rested for a long moment on Chadwick's heavy double cartridge belt, and on the brass rims of the shells snugged in the loop. He raised his eyes to the cattle king's and the look in them was inscrutable.

"Yes, I'll come," he said quietly. "I think we ought to have an interesting session."

Amado Capistrano had already accepted the rancher's invitation.

Glancing toward the door, Hatfield saw a lithe, dark

little man enter the saloon. A moment later he left the table with a word of excuse and sauntered through the swinging doors. Outside he waited until Pancho, the Yaqui tracker, joined him.

"They ride tonight, *Capitan,*" Pancho whispered, his eyes snapping with excitement. "All will be there tonight, or nearly all. Cartina himself will be there, and perhaps the other of whom you spoke. We strike, *Capitan?*"

Jim Hatfield glanced toward the distant hilltops, and Pancho, eagerly reading his expression, gazed upon the face of the Lone Wolf, a bleak, terrible face in which were set eyes that glittered coldly as frosted dagger points under a winter sun.

Again the Ranger and the tracker rode into the hills. On the crest of a long ridge they separated, Pancho making his way to the cavern mouth in the hollow. Hatfield rode to where the conveyor buckets clicked past the gloomy cleft in the cliff. He concealed Goldy in a thicket on the banks of a little stream, where he could have grass and water, and entered the cleft. On the lip of the ghastly pit he crouched, listening to the murmur of the far off water, which came up from the vast depths.

Hatfield was listening for another sound—a sound that would tell him Pancho had successfully completed his dangerous task. He could visualize the little tracker, creeping silently as a lizard toward the mighty mass of rock which overhung the cave mouth. He could see him, in his mind's eye, counting the evil faced riders who passed beneath the gloomy arch to enter the cave. He could see the Yaqui tense as the last one vanished in the dark depths—see him strike a light and fire the end of the long fuse that led to the hidden dynamite. His palms grew clammily moist as he thought of the mighty mass of stone thundering down to block the entrance to the cavern and make of it a living tomb.

"They've got it coming," he muttered as he fingered the length of fuse which was attached to the dynamite planted along the surface of the crumbling ledge. "It'll be good for them to think for a spell that they really *are* buried alive without any water or food."

Suddenly he tensed and his muscles swelled like iron bands. Down the gloomy aisle of the corridor drifted a sullen boom followed by a rumbling thunder. Hatfield could almost hear the cries of terror and see the sudden rush toward the narrow corridor which led past the pit and to the cleft in the cliff by the conveyor line. Grimly he stooped and set fire to the end of the fuse. It sputtered, smoked, and then burned steadily.

Hatfield stood up, and instantly hurled himself sideways and down. He had sensed rather than seen or heard the menace creeping toward him through the clammy dark. He was flat on the ground when the gun flashed fire and a bullet whistled through the space his body had occupied the instant before. He shot forward in a streaking dive and crashed into the man who had fired the shot.

He heard the gun clatter to the stone floor. Then

arms like bands of steel wrapped about his body and he was lifted off his feet.

With all his strength he lashed out viciously. His fist crunched against flesh and bone with a shock that jarred his arm to the shoulder. The other's hold loosened slightly and the Ranger regained his feet.

Mightily, the two powerful men wrestled, reeling, swaying, their breath coming in panting gasps. Never in his life had the Lone Wolf encountered such superhuman strength. The abnormally long, gnarled arms crushed his chest until it was as if a red hot clasp of iron encircled it. He bowed his back and resisted to the last atom.

Backward the other forced him. Suddenly, with a terrible chill of horror, he felt a foot slip over the edge of the pit. Another instant and he would be hurled into the awful depths. With a final mighty effort he sent his opponent reeling away from the lip of the gulf. Then, utterly unexpectedly, he hurled himself down upon his back, gripping the other's forearms at the same instant and kicking upward with all the strength of his sinewy legs.

Caught by the mighty thrust of those pistoning legs, the other man shot into the air. Hatfield jerked down on the forearms at the same instant and then let go.

The squat, powerful body of Hatfield's assailant shot through the air, cleared the edge of the pit and hurtled downward with an awful scream of terror and despair. Up from the depths came the cry, growing thin with distance—then the faint whisper of a splash.

Sheriff Branch Horton, his days of murderous treachery done, was taking a long, long one-way trip to Hell!

Gasping and panting, Hatfield scrambled to his feet. Numbly he remembered the dynamite and the burning fuse. He staggered away from the edge of the pit, shambling toward the outer air and safety.

With a clap of thunder and a lurid reddish glare, the dynamite let go. Down into the pit crashed yard after yard of the ledge, making the way past the gulf unpassable, imprisoning the men who came yelling down the long corridor from the great central cavern.

But Jim Hatfield did not hear the thudding feet nor the howls of despair. Near the mouth of the cleft he lay, silent and motionless, with the acrid fumes of the burned powder wisping about his white face.

Chapter XVIII

JIM HATFIELD regained consciousness to feel the drip of cold water on his face. Opening his reluctant lids, he glanced up into the dark, anxious face of Pancho, the little tracker. The Yaqui's black eyes glowed warmly as Hatfield struggled to a sitting position.

"*Capitan!* You live!" he exclaimed.

"I'm not so sure of it," the Ranger replied. "Feel as though I ought to be dead. What happened?"

"I know not," replied the Yaqui. "After making sure that the entrance to the cavern was blocked securely, I hurried across the ridge as you directed. I found you here, pale and still. I thought you to be dead."

The whinny of a horse brought Hatfield's head up around. Tied to a tree was a sturdy roan, Sheriff Branch Horton's horse. Sunlight was shimmering on his black coat.

The sight of that sunlight, pouring almost straight down from the brassy-blue sky, sent remembrance crashing through the Ranger's mind. He struggled to his feet and headed, somewhat shakily, for the thicket in which he had left his tall golden sorrel.

"Unhitch that black horse and ride him," he called to Pancho. "You and I have got some riding to do, Pancho! If we're not a long way the other side of these hills by noon, a mighty fine man is going to die!"

Together they rode across the hills, the Yaqui clinging like a burr to the unaccustomed saddle. They drummed on as the blazing sun arched upward into the sky toward the misty blue west. It was well past noon when the white buildings of John Chadwick's Circle C came into view.

Hatfield and Pancho circled the apparently deserted ranch buildings, approaching them from the rear by way of a thick grove of burr oaks. No sound greeted them as they crept stealthily through the closeset tree trunks.

At the edge of the grove, several feet from the ranchhouse, they paused. Then the Yaqui crept on, a drifting shadow that seemed to lack real substance. He flattened himself against the wall as footsteps sounded inside the house. A door opened and Edwards, Chadwick's foreman, stepped into view, a rifle in his hands. His quick eye caught the loom of Hatfield's tall form amid the trees and he flung a rifle to his shoulder.

For a tense instant, disaster hovered in the balance. The crash of the report, no matter who fired first, would warn any other inmates of the house. Hatfield's hands had moved with blurring speed and the muzzles of his Colts yawned hungrily at Edwards, but he hesitated to pull trigger.

In that split instant, Pancho drifted along the side of the ranchhouse like a swirl of dusky smoke. His sinewy arm rose and fell. Something gleamed brightly in the sunlight, and was dimmed by a reddish stain.

Edwards' body fell forward as Pancho wrenched his knife from between the foreman's shoulder blades. The Yaqui caught the limp body in his wiry arms and eased it silently to the ground, preventing the rifle from clattering at the same instant. Hatfield reached him in three giant strides. He motioned to the door which Edwards left ajar. They slipped through and moved silently along the shadowy hall toward the front of the house, from which came voices. Crouched just outside a second door, they peered through a crack.

Seated on one side of the room was Amado Capistrano. His arms were bound and he was tied to his chair. On his handsome face was an expression of faint amusement as he stared into the flashing eyes of John Chadwick, who stood facing him. His glance strayed across the room to Joseph Bowers, his mine superintendent, and his clear eyes mirrored contempt.

"Yes, you're not going to live long, you wriggle-backed greaser sidewinder," Chadwick was saying. "You crossed me once too often. I'm doing for you as soon as your Ranger friend gets here, and for him, too. Folks are going to think you killed each other. It won't be hard to fix it that way."

For the first time Capistrano's face showed concern.

"Let the Ranger alone, Chadwick," he said in his musical voice. "Murdering him won't get you any-thing."

Chadwick snarled an oath.

"He's in my way," he grated. "The time will come," he boasted, "when his kind will come eating out of my hand, when I get things going right in this state. Right now when they get in my way, I squash them like I would a horned toad."

He shouted over his shoulder:

"Hey, Ed, aren't the boys riding in yet?"

"I don't think the boys will ever come riding in again, Chadwick," drawled a quiet voice from the doorway.

Chadwick whirled in amazement to face the doorway. The Lone Wolf stood there, towering in his great height. His face was as cold as wind-beaten granite, his eyes like icy water torturing under frozen snow. The eyes shifted suddenly and his slim hands moved with blinding speed. From the muzzle of one black Colt wisped a spiral of blue smoke. The room echoed to the roar of the explosion.

Joseph Bowers reeled sideways, his half drawn gun clattering to the floor. Retching and choking, he writhed on the woven rug, his face ghastly, blood pouring from the gaping wound in his chest. Hatfield holstered his smoking gun and turned his terrible eyes on Chadwick once more.

"I'm giving you a full chance, Chadwick, you murdering skunk," he said, his voice deadly in its softness. "More than you gave Dick Webb or Ed Shafter. Get going, Chadwick! Reach for those mismated guns of yours—the forty-five and the thirty-two-twenty. Those guns gave you away, Chadwick. Dick and Ed had holes in their heads made by different caliber bullets. Reach for them, Chadwick—or come along peaceably and be hanged!"

For an instant John Chadwick seemed to hesitate. Then blind, ungovernable fury blackened his face and his guns came roaring from their shoulder holsters.

Through a haze of powder smoke he saw Jim Hatfield standing straight and tall, blood trickling down one bronzed cheek. Blood was welling in Chadwick's mouth. His breast was crushed and shattered by the heavy slugs that had hammered the bone to bits. Forward he fell, toppling slowly, to lie silent and motionless at the Lone Wolf's feet.

"Dyson can get a posse together and get into that cave to haul out that nest of snakes we've got penned up there," Hatfield told Amado Capistrano after the other had been released.

"Dyson's honest—dumb, but honest. He didn't

know Horton was in cahoots with Chadwick. He didn't know Chadwick was the prize crook of the district. Yes, I knew Chadwick planned to kill us both when he got us here. I was coming prepared for him, but things worked out to make me late."

He smiled briefly.

"Well, it all ended okay so that's that," he said. "Now you can go on back to your business of sending sick kids to hospitals and planning schools for the well ones, and helping folks who are in trouble. Things will be better in this district now, and here's hoping you end up owning all of the old Capistrano home ranch before you get through!"

Several days later, Jim Hatfield reported in full to grim old Captain McDowell at Ranger headquarters.

"A lie Horton and Chadwick told gave me my first real line on them," he told Cap Bill. "That day I met them at the Cibola mine, they said they'd been in the hills all night. They were mighty anxious to have me believe they *had* been in the hills. They hadn't!"

"How'd you know they hadn't?" Cap Bill asked. Hatfield chuckled.

"They were all covered with dust, sir, and it wasn't the red dust of the hills," he explained. "It was the gray alkali dust of the desert. They'd been around the hills to meet the rest of their outfit from down Mexico way.

"Then when I sent telegrams and traced down Bowers' activities since the time he got fired for being drunk and miscalculating that bridge job, I found out he'd been associating with Chadwick for a long time. Bowers had a penitentiary record for crooked work. Chadwick got him pardoned because he could use him. Bowers was a smart engineer, but he couldn't keep straight."

He paused a moment, rolling a cigarette with the slim, bronzed fingers of one hand.

"Chadwick's scheme was a lulu!" he exclaimed. "He wasn't going in for the plain ordinary brand of banditry. He was planning to clean out the whole Tamarra Valley.

"He drilled those men of his like they were an army. Pedro Cartina was his front man, who took all the blame and did the strutting. Chadwick was the brains. Horton was another blockhead he'd raised up from nothing."

He lit the cigarette and exhaled a long ribbon of smoke.

"The ore stealing idea was Bowers', and it was a smart one," he continued. "Chadwick was sending the ore to his Humboldt mine and slipping it into his stamp mill. No wonder the Humboldt was doing well. Holding up the stage and stealing his own insured payroll wasn't so bad, either, and they even took a whack at the bank, and nearly got away with a fat haul.

"Some of the gang," he continued, "were real bad men, and those that weren't Cartina scared into doing whatever was wanted, like that poor little devil I picked up in the desert. He was a spy in the Cibola mine, sending reports when high-grade ore was coming out. Giving him one of those Government model rifles was a mistake.

"Webb and Shafter caught on to what was going on, particularly Shafter, and Chadwick wiped them out. It was seeing those different sized loops on Chadwick's cartridge belt that cinched my case on him. Well, sir, I guess that about clears up everything, doesn't it?"

"Uh-huh," agreed Cap Bill, "excepting what you're going to do with that little saddle colored Indian you brought along with you."

"Oh, Pancho," grinned Hatfield. "Pancho's the best tracker to ever come out of Mexico, and he sure is dependable."

"Better take him with you where I'm sending you next, then," remarked Captain Bill drily. "From what I hear, there isn't much dependable in that district, and you've got a tough job ahead of you, if you ever had one!"

"Yes, sir!" replied the Lone Wolf, his eyes sunny with pleasurable anticipation. Then the Ranger's eyes turned somber, but with a quiet satisfaction in their depths.

Jim Hatfield was thinking of a lonely grave on a hillside overlooking the Huachuca Trail where the winds whispered softly through the cathedral aisles of the pines and a tall yucca lifted high on its single stem a great cluster of drooping lily-white blossoms that swayed gently in the breeze like a swung censer.

He knew that Ed Shafter could sleep peacefully now.

Center Point Publishing
600 Brooks Road ● PO Box 1
Thorndike ME 04986-0001 USA

(207) 568-3717

US & Canada:
1 800 929-9108
www.centerpointlargeprint.com